PE

BERGERAC AND

Andrew Saville is the p̶⟶⟶⟶⟶ award-winning
crime writer who lives in Gloucestershire.

Other titles in this series:

Already published

ANDREW SAVILLE

BERGERAC
AND THE
TRAITOR'S
CHILD

PENGUIN BOOKS

PENGUIN BOOKS

Published by the Penguin Group

27 Wrights Lane, London w8 5tz, England

Viking Penguin Inc., 40 West 23rd Street, New York, New York 10010, USA

Penguin Books Australia Ltd, Ringwood, Victoria, Australia

Penguin Books Canada Ltd, 2801 John Street, Markham, Ontario, Canada l3r 1b4

Penguin Books (NZ) Ltd, 182–190 Wairau Road, Auckland 10, New Zealand

Penguin Books Ltd, Registered Offices: Harmondsworth, Middlesex, England

Published in Penguin Books 1988

Filmset in 10/12 Linotron Baskerville

by Centracet

Made and printed in Great Britain by

Richard Clay Ltd, Bungay, Suffolk

It started, old George Crozier used to say, with a man and a woman in a garden. Just like the Book of Genesis, except in this case the man doubled up as the serpent.

Murder, he claimed, violence and greed all sprang from a seed that was planted in the big garden of the house on Wellington Road. Thanks to Nullhausen, they could even put a date and a time to it.

Bergerac didn't agree. Old George was a bit of a philosopher and tended to make life seem neater than it was. Any starting-point you picked out of the past was, in a sense, randomly selected. You could say that this business went back further than forty-odd years – to an English art student in Paris in the 1880s, for example; or to the rise of Adolf Hitler; or to whatever incident made Patrice Marigny into the man he later became.

But one thing was certain. The Jersey States Police had no time for philosophical speculation, least of all in the records section. They wanted facts, reasons and – if unavoidable – well-supported theories. When Bergerac came to compile the full report, he had to begin somewhere. The Bureau des Etrangers needed to know about the roots of the affair – which meant going back to the last, bitter spring of the German Occupation of Jersey. Maybe George was right: the man and the woman in the garden was as good a place as any to start. At least the incident and the events that surrounded it were well documented.

There were the official records, of course, both German and English. There were all the books and pamphlets that had been published since the war. There were the archives in the possession of the Société Jersiaise, the Channel Islands Occupation Society and the Channel Islands Historical Trust. There were private letters and diaries. Among the latter, Nullhausen's journal was particularly valuable – he was Marigny's professional shadow for the whole of the Jersey posting; the Germans never really trusted the Vichy French.

Best of all, there were the living memories of the people who had been there. Every month the number of eye-witnesses dwindled as age took its toll. But the ones who were left remembered their life under the Germans with a vividness that Bergerac found shocking. Nearly half a century had failed to heal the scars or, in some cases, purge the anger or the guilt. Often it was difficult to persuade them to talk about it: had it been possible, they would have liked to forget. But one old woman – now in the psychiatric unit at the General Hospital – talked too much. Her memories were the most vivid of all.

So the report began with a man and a woman in a garden. The material fell naturally into two sections – then and now. Some of it had to be guesswork, but surprisingly little. Even Detective Chief Inspector Barney Crozier had to admit that.

PART ONE
THEN – SPRING
1945

CHAPTER
I

'The old bastard's hidden it somewhere,' the woman said. She stroked the sleeve of the man's leather coat. 'But you'll find it, Patrice, won't you?'

Marigny patted her hand. 'It shouldn't be too difficult.' His English was fluent and his accent was so good that he was often taken for a Londoner. 'Just a matter of asking the right questions in the right way.'

She looked over her shoulder to check once again that they were out of sight of the house.

'He's an obstinate old devil,' she said softly.

'We're used to dealing with that.' Marigny glanced quickly at her. 'But we'll have to kill him afterwards. We can't leave him to talk. It'll take a bit of organization.'

'But you can do it, surely?'

'Oh, yes. But it would have been easier a year ago. We could have shipped him off to Auschwitz instead.'

'But what about *us*?' The woman's voice was shrill with panic.

'Us?' Marigny seemed more interested in the row of cabbages than in the woman by his side. 'We'll manage, *chérie*. When the war is over, I may have to lie low for a while. I have my plans. As for you, your husband will come back. The gallant hero himself. You will bask in his reflected glory. It will be easy.'

'Easy?' Her laugh was bitter. 'God knows what they'll do to women like me.'

'To Jerrybags?' he asked with a hint of amusement. 'That's what they call the – '

'I know what the word means.'

'In your case, my dear, it would be inaccurate. I am French, you remember.'

'Do you think that will make a difference?' It was a mild, spring day, but she shivered.

'Stop tormenting yourself. Nobody knows about us.'

'I can't be sure. *She* might have guessed.'

'Who?'

'Little Miss Butter-wouldn't-melt-in-my-mouth.'

Marigny shrugged, bored with the subject. 'In any case, we will only be separated for a short time.'

'But how long will it be?'

'Who knows? A few months? A year, perhaps. Then I will come back for you.' He pulled out his case and offered her a cigarette. 'Now, my dear, we must talk about tonight. There is another way you can help me.'

She smoked the cigarette with obsessive concentration while he told her what he wanted her to do.

'Well?' he said finally. 'You can manage that?'

'All right,' she said in a dull voice. 'If it's important. What does it matter?'

She stubbed out the half-smoked cigarette and concealed the butt in an empty matchbox.

Marigny stroked her cheek. 'I must go. Until tonight, my love.'

Desperation suddenly overlaid the apathy on her face. 'Patrice, there is something else – '

'I had no idea Tillersland had so many vegetables,' Marigny interrupted. 'I must send a detail round to collect them.'

'Patrice! Will you listen?'

He looked at her for a long moment. He was a lightly built man with a mobile, expressive face. She guessed he was in his forties, but he looked younger. Sometimes she thought he had missed his vocation: he should have been an actor.

'What is it, my dear?'

The words were mild enough, but something in his face warned her to be careful.

'My . . . my period's late. And there are other signs. I think I may be pregnant.'

'In that case . . .' He hesitated, choosing his words with care. 'Let us hope your husband comes home soon. You might find it inconvenient to have a little bastard. Especially if I am the father.'

'But what am I to do?'

'You can bring the baby with you,' he said with a smile. 'When I come back after the war, I shall collect you both. Satisfied?'

'Oh, Patrice – '

He turned and left her, weeping silently among the cabbages.

Nullhausen was waiting for Marigny in the car.

His gloved hands played restlessly with the steering-wheel. Every few seconds he glanced in the rear-view mirror.

Marigny had made him park the Mercedes at the bottom of the hill, in St Saviour's Road. There was no point, he had said, in advertising the Gestapo's interest in the house on Wellington Road.

The Mercedes was even more conspicuous than it would have been earlier in the war. By 1945 there were few cars on the roads of Jersey.

Nullhausen knew that Marigny was right about the need for discretion, but nevertheless the Frenchman's absence made him uneasy. There might be repercussions.

Marigny had been seconded to the Gestapo on Jersey some time after the Germans had occupied Vichy France. He had formerly been a high-ranking officer in the *Milice*, the secret police of the Vichy regime. Subsequently he had worked for the Gestapo in Lyons. He came with the highest recommendations.

The authorities had decided to transfer Marigny to Jersey for several reasons. His police skills were proven beyond doubt; he spoke perfect English and German, as well as his native French; and he was too useful a man to leave idle.

But still his nationality left a question mark over him. That was why the authorities, in their wisdom, had decided that Kurt Nullhausen should be Marigny's subordinate. Every fortnight, as Marigny was well aware, Nullhausen reported on his superior to the island's Gestapo chief in Havre de Pas. It was an arrangement that Nullhausen detested. His one aim was to survive this beastly war in one piece so that he could get back to his wife in Hamburg and his job in the civil police. Since he had been assigned to Marigny, he felt that he had become too well known; anonymity was safer.

And Marigny was the sort of man who brought trouble to those around him.

The Frenchman's elegant figure appeared in the mirror, turning out of Wellington Road. Nullhausen felt a stab of envy: he himself was small and plump; his suits always looked baggy and crumpled the moment he put them on.

Marigny's leather coat was open, revealing his grey, double-breasted suit in all its glory. In one hand he held a cigarette; in the other was his cane. Nullhausen had seen Marigny use the cane on suspects.

Marigny opened the passenger door and stepped gracefully into the car.

'Success, sir?' Nullhausen asked. He was invariably polite to Marigny; the man had a lot of powerful friends.

'My source confirms it,' Marigny said. 'I think we'll go in tonight.'

'Is that wise, sir? In view of the situation?'

Nullhausen waved his hand in a gesture that silently

embraced the fact that the German army had lost the war and the Führer was doomed.

'My dear Kurt!' Marigny raised his eyebrows. 'Surely you are not suggesting that we fail to do our duty?'

'But a radio – these days it's such a minor matter.'

'It's not just an illegal crystal set. No, there's a strong possibility that the man's a Jew. It's our moral and official duty to investigate.'

'Yes, sir,' Nullhausen agreed without enthusiasm. 'But – in the circumstances – might it not be a little undiplomatic? Perhaps we should merely put him under surveillance.'

It was a bold speech for Nullhausen, and he regretted the words as soon as they were out of his mouth. But a man had to take precautions where his own safety was concerned. God alone knew what the Allies would do when they had won the war. If half the rumours were true, they would have plenty to be angry about. If Marigny wanted to spend the rest of his life as some sort of war criminal, that was his affair. But Nullhausen had no desire to be dragged down with him.

Marigny shook his head. 'I see your point, Kurt, naturally.' His face was uncomfortably sardonic; Nullhausen avoided his superior's eyes. 'But I've made up my mind. Quite apart from Tillersland himself, we have to consider the propaganda value. The islanders are getting complacent. They need to be reminded that we still have teeth.'

'You're right, sir,' Nullhausen said quickly. 'Where now? Headquarters?'

Marigny nodded. 'Besides,' he added, 'there's a vegetable garden behind that high wall. And a lot of stores in the house. Quite illegal. We need the food, Kurt. When did you last have a square meal?'

Nullhausen's mouth watered at the memory. As he drove carefully through St Helier, he had two thoughts in his mind. The first was that the sooner he got all this down in his journal, the better; the journal was his secret insurance against Germany losing the war – it was a laborious defence of his inglorious and undesired secondment to the Gestapo.

The second thought was in the form of a question. Why was Marigny sticking his neck out? At this stage of the war, his interest in a minor law-breaker just didn't make sense, even if the culprit really was Jewish. It wasn't even possible to deport the man, for Jersey was cut off from the rest of the world; its very survival was dependent on Red Cross food cargoes.

Nor did Nullhausen believe that Marigny was actuated by a sense of duty: his devotion to the ideals of Fascism was solely the result of his devotion to himself. The Reich had failed to conquer the world as planned. There was no longer any need for Marigny to obey to the letter some of its more absurd laws.

To put the question another way, if Tillersland were arrested, what would be in it for Patrice Marigny?

Before the war Henry Tillersland's garden had been famous for its roses.

As the old man cycled up the drive, he remembered the roses with affection. Even now his garden gave him pleasure. He dismounted and, leaning on his bicycle, stared at his land

We are all peasants at heart, he thought; *and it took a war to make me realize it.* The thought was followed by another: *Soon I shall be able to grow roses again.*

In the old days he had won several prizes for his roses at horticultural shows. His rivals used to hint that he employed his specialized knowledge as a chemist to produce those miraculously regular and superbly coloured blooms. Some thought he had a secret formula for his fertilizer; others believed it was all in the sprays he used. It was all nonsense, of course.

But for the last five years there had been few roses in the garden at Wellington Road. Young George Crozier, the gardener, had been among the first to enlist in the British army in 1939, so Tillersland had to cope with an acre of garden by himself. It was impossible to find a replacement for George: when Jersey was partly evacuated just before the Germans invaded in June 1940, young men of military age were encouraged to leave for the mainland, along with the women and children. There was work for them elsewhere.

Tillersland himself had a good reason to go with the evacuees, but he told his friends he was too old to move just because an upstart Austrian house painter had taken fancy to the Channel Islands. There was little danger, since the islands had been declared a demilitarized zone; and, in any case, the British would soon send the Germans packing.

While he waited for this to happen, he dug up most of his roses and all of his lawn. It was hard work for an old man, but worth it in the end. In place of grass and flowers he planted vegetables. As the food shortages began to bite, vegetables were worth their weight in gold. His luck held: marauding troops and foreign workers rarely found their way into his garden.

The Germans stayed for longer than anyone had thought possible. At first they tried to make it a model occupation – the Führer wanted to show the British people that he could behave like a gentleman to the conquered, especially when the conquered included decent Aryan stock whom he would have preferred to be his allies rather than his enemies. Hitler took a personal interest in the Channel Islands for the simple reason that they were the only part of the British Empire he succeeded in occupying. He poured troops and *matériel* into them; the islands became an important part of the Atlantic Wall that defended the Greater Reich.

As the war progressed, the Occupation became harsher for occupiers and conquered alike. When the Allies opened the second front in 1944, conditions grew even worse. The unpleasant irony was not lost on the islanders: in this war they seemed perpetually doomed to be among the losers. The Germans were no longer able to supply the islands from mainland France. The islanders and the slave labour force were the first to feel the pinch. By April 1945 the *Wehrmacht* garrisons were going hungry. Horse-flesh sausages and rotten potatoes were a poor diet, even when supplemented by nettle soup and stolen turnips. Rumour had it that most of the troops were unfit to fight; their ailments ranged from tuberculosis to insanity and many of them had died of disease on their fortress island of Jersey.

Henry Tillersland knew he was fortunate. Despite the war, he was still a wealthy man. It was an unpleasant but inevitable truth that the Occupation was less intolerable for the rich than for the poor. Tillersland could afford to buy what luxuries the black market had to offer. At first he had been too scrupulous to take advantage of this, but after the first year the black market had become a useful aid to survival – not only for himself, but for Elsie, Marie and their families.

The produce of his garden was some compensation for the increasingly meagre rations doled out by the authorities. He had few domestic cares, for a cook and a maid looked after the large Victorian house. Many of his friends' staff had been lured away by the Germans, who paid double wages; Tillersland doubted whether either of his servants would have left, but he had raised their wages to make absolutely sure.

He had only himself to worry about. Elizabeth, his wife, had died just before the war. Their only child was somewhere in the British army; David might not be safe, but at least he was a free man. Apart from brief and occasional messages through the Red Cross, Tillersland had heard nothing from him for nearly five years.

No – he had to admit that by and large he had had a relatively easy war. True, the Germans had impounded his car; on the other hand, he was fortunate enough to possess a bicycle, and cycling helped to keep him fit.

The war must end soon, perhaps in a few weeks. That was common knowledge on Jersey, where home-made crystal sets, Tillersland's among them, monitored the news bulletins of the BBC. It was unlikely that the Germans would defend the Channel Islands once the rest of the Reich had surrendered. There would be no point. Besides, how could their underfed and isolated troops put up much resistance?

Liberation must come soon. The roses would return.

He wheeled the bicycle round the house to what had once been the coach-house. He padlocked the rear wheel to a ring on the wall and took the further precaution of locking the door of the coach-house behind him. You couldn't be too careful. There was so much theft; unfortunately, islanders were sometimes involved, as well as the soldiers and the slave labour. He had noticed that the war was a forcing house for human nature: it made the bad worse and the good better.

His boots were muddy, so he went into the house by the back door. He removed them in the scullery. Elsie and Marie were chattering in the kitchen; he called out to let them know he was back.

They were good girls, he thought. Both of them had husbands serving in the Hampshire Regiment. Marriage was another casualty of war. God knew what might have happened to them if he hadn't been able to keep them here. They were good-looking, and the temptation to fraternize with the enemy, particularly in the early years of the Occupation, must have been difficult to resist if you were poor.

Marie came into the scullery. 'I brought your slippers, sir.' She glanced down at his feet. 'And you'd better change those socks. They're soaking wet.'

'I will, my dear,' he said meekly. 'Is tea ready?'

She nodded. 'Elsie's just opened our last packet. They'd better liberate us soon, that's all I can say.'

At night the gates were locked.

She was already in bed when Tillersland trudged down the drive to shut them in for the night. She heard his footsteps returning, dragging on the gravel as if he were too weary to walk. She tried not to feel sorry for him and managed to succeed.

It was only nine o'clock. She had a long wait in front of her.

The old man used not to bother with the gates. But last year there had been an ugly incident involving a group of Russian prisoners of war who were foraging on behalf of their *Wehrmacht* guards. It might have been much worse if a patrol from the *Feldgendarmerie* had not intervened.

Patrice had told her to wait until everyone was asleep. These days, they all went to bed early. There was no electricity at present, and the old man found reading by candlelight difficult.

Shortly after midnight she decided it was safe to get up. She pulled on her dressing-gown and tiptoed along the landing to the open door of the attic bedroom next to hers.

The room was in darkness. All she could hear was breathing, with the even rhythm of a deep sleeper. She stole away to the head of the stairs. There she paused for a few seconds. It had to be done.

'*It will be much better,*' Patrice had said this afternoon, '*if he knows nothing until we arrive at his bedside. Do not be afraid. Trust me, little one.*'

She crept down the first flight of stairs. She had familiarized herself years before with the treads and floorboards that creaked. It had always been convenient to be able to move quietly about the house.

By now her eyes had grown accustomed to the dark. On the main landing she stopped by the closed door of her master's room. She would have liked to have made sure that he was asleep, but, if she went in, the click of the latch might wake him. She compromised by peering through the keyhole. Tillersland had blown out his candle. It was safe to go on.

Once downstairs she picked up the key from the salver on the hall table and slipped through the green baize door that led to the kitchen, the pantries and the scullery. Although it would have been quicker, she had decided not to go out of the front door because the heavy bolts and the two locks might make a noise. Tillersland's room was directly over the hall, and, to make matters worse, the old man was a light sleeper.

In the kitchen she stumbled into the haybox in which tomorrow's turnip stew was cooking. A muffled gasp escaped her. She waited a full minute before moving on.

Outside it was much colder, but in her relief she hardly noticed. She walked quickly to the gates, clutching the key to her breast; she kept parallel to the drive and avoided stepping on the gravel. Tomorrow she would have to clean the mud from her slippers; it was a small price to pay for silence.

The gates loomed up ahead. She might have been alone in a blacked-out world. The only sound was the distant drone of a plane's engine. Her heart thumped uncomfortably in her chest.

She eased back the two bolts. She searched with the tips of her fingers for the keyhole. Part of her hoped that she wouldn't find it. But it was too late to change her mind. It was too late to change anything.

The key slid into the lock. She gripped it and tried to summon up the willpower to turn it. Her skin was slippery with sweat, cooling rapidly in the night air. She thought she heard a movement on the other side, in Wellington Road. The scrape of a leather sole on the pavement? Her nostrils twitched as they caught the scent of tobacco. *God – what wouldn't I do for a cigarette?*

The yearning for tobacco removed the last of her hesitation.

'Patrice?' she whispered. 'Patrice?'

CHAPTER
2

The first that Henry Tillersland knew of it was when he heard them coming up the stairs.

One moment he was thinking about pesticides, the next he was struggling to resist the tide of helplessness and fear that threatened to drown him.

Fortunately, he was still awake, lying on his back with his head propped up on three pillows. In his old age, an unbroken night's sleep had become a rarity. He slept more lightly; an uncomfortable position woke him more easily; he needed to go to the lavatory more often. In consequence, he frequently dropped into a doze during the day.

The footsteps came steadily closer. They were not in any hurry; they made no effort to conceal themselves. They belonged to men who had neither legal nor moral qualms about what they were doing – and no doubts about their ability to do it.

Tillersland felt curiously detached from it all. His mind seemed to fragment into a mosaic of different thoughts. In the last five years he had often wondered how he would react if it came to this. In a sense he was more afraid of acting shamefully than of the Gestapo or the *Feldgendarmerie* themselves. It was a relief to find that his mind was still working. Had it been possible, he would have liked to have timed his pulse; it would have been interesting to know if the rate had accelerated.

Simultaneously his brain was dealing with another matter. The intruders hadn't broken down the front door or smashed the window or rung the bell. He hadn't heard them on the drive or opening the gate.

The implication was monstrous: someone must have let them in.

Elsie? Marie?

It was impossible. They were good girls. He had cared for them as they had cared for him.

But how else could they know – ?

No one else came to the house, not now. His friends had left the island; they had died or they had found the effort of keeping up the acquaintance no longer worth while. Friendships, like roses, demanded care and attention if they were to survive. The war had forced Tillersland to husband his energies. He had made no new friends.

So – Elsie or Marie? He hoped he knew the answer. If he were wrong, he had miscalculated badly, and he would have to pay for the mistake. So, for that matter, would David. If he came back from the war.

Even as Tillersland was thinking this, he was moving. The mind lost itself in an ill-disciplined welter of thoughts while the body obediently followed the routine that the mind had pre-ordained so long ago. He had planned for this eventuality, rehearsing the actions until they had become second nature; but he had also made the rash assumption that he would have more time at his disposal. It was infuriating that his muscles were so stiff, that age and cold had made his limbs so clumsy. He yearned for the unthinking physical co-ordination of youth.

It was too dark to see what he was doing. In any case, he was effectively blind without his glasses. One groping hand knocked over the glass of water; it fell from the bedside table and shattered on the floor.

They must have heard. The footsteps outside speeded up. Pray God the door would hold them for the few precious seconds he needed.

His hand flailed through the darkness and found the

brass catch on the bedside cupboard. He tugged at it with increasing desperation. The cupboard rocked.

They had reached the landing. Dear God – had they sent an entire army for one old man?

The cupboard opened with a jerk that sent his candle-stick to join the splinters of glass on the floor.

Someone tried the handle on the bedroom door. *How did they know which was my room?* Then there were three booming blows on the panels – it sounded as if the man were slapping the wood with the flat of his hand.

'Open up,' a voice said in English. 'Gestapo.'

Tillersland cleared his throat. 'One moment,' he said. 'I am coming.'

To his disgust, his voice came out as a quavering bleat. Old age brought so many humiliations in its train.

His fingertips touched the envelope. He pulled it out of the cupboard and fumbled at the unsealed flap.

The hammer blow came without warning. The house shuddered. Wood splintered, but the door held up. Thank God it was solid Victorian oak.

The flap of the envelope came up. He shook the contents into the palm of his hand and threw himself back against the pillows. Another blow shook the building.

Let them come. I am ready now.

The door bucked on its hinges. Light flickered around the frame and through the hole in the top, left-hand panel. Suddenly the hinges gave way as their screws were ripped from the jamb. The entire door fell forward and clattered on to the floor of the bedroom.

The room was full of men and torchlight. He thought there were four of them, but at first it was difficult to be sure. Trench coats and hats made them anonymous. One of them carried the sledgehammer across his chest.

The smallest of the four detached himself from the group and came towards the bed. In one hand he held a torch, in the other an automatic.

The torch found his face. Tillersland was dazzled by the glare. He threw up his hands to protect his eyes.

'Henry Tillersland?' the man said quietly. 'You're under arrest.'

Tillersland slowly lowered his hands. 'Would you mind if I put in my teeth?'

Nullhausen was in a quandary.

Marigny had herded Tillersland and the two maids into the drawing-room. All three of them had been allowed to put on their dressing-gowns, but they were obviously cold.

The girls huddled together on one of the sofas. Both of them were pretty young things, even without make-up – a bit gaunt, naturally; but nowadays most of the islanders were.

The question was: which of the two was the traitor?

Marigny had declined to tell Nullhausen the name of his bit of skirt; and Nullhausen had been wise enough to back off. The orders had been to treat them both in the same way: as the potentially suspicious employees of a suspected subversive and racial deviant. That made sense: it was a standard police tactic not to reveal the identity of your stool-pigeon unless you had to; if carefully handled, a reliable informer could have a long and useful life.

One of the two gorillas was standing by the door; Marigny had taken the other one to help him search the house. It annoyed and puzzled Nullhausen that Marigny had left him to do the preliminary form-filling; usually one of the gorillas would have done a menial job like that.

Name – date and place of birth – occupation – marital status – number of children, if any – colour of eyes and hair – height and weight.

Nullhausen's nib scratched on the cheap official paper. All these bloody forms, he thought – one for every conceivable occasion in life or death, with duplicates and triplicates to meet every possible contingency that the bureaucrats could imagine. When the Reich finally collapsed, they could bury the ruins under a mound of paper.

He signed the third form and glanced again at the women on the sofa. Really very tasty, even now when they were scared out of their heads. Given half a chance, he wouldn't mind meeting them on a happier occasion. Not that they would ever look at him as women looked at Patrice Marigny. Only Gretl had ever looked at Kurt Nullhausen; that was why he had married her.

Mrs Elsie Fishguard and Mrs Marie Crozier; both with husbands serving in the British army; both childless and in their early twenties. They even looked alike – to the extent that they might have been sisters.

The old man was sitting like a statue in the wing armchair by the empty fireplace. Suddenly he raised his hand, like a schoolchild asking permission to speak.

'Yes?' Nullhausen said. 'What is it?'

He kept his voice neutral because the gorilla was listening.

Tillersland cleared his throat. 'Mrs Crozier and Mrs Fishguard are very cold,' he mumbled in German; Marigny had not allowed him to put in his dentures. 'Would you permit them to get dressed?' He swallowed, the Adam's apple rising and falling in the skinny neck, and added, 'Perhaps we might even have some tea?'

Tea – the Englishman's first refuge in times of crisis. Nullhausen wondered if they still had real tea and not some herbal tisane. Actually, it wasn't a bad idea – he was feeling chilly himself. And warmer clothes were, on the surface at least, a perfectly reasonable request.

The gorilla by the door took a step forward as if he were about to speak. Nullhausen scowled at him. Karl was so stupid; apart from physical strength, stupidity was his only qualification for the job he did. The fool hadn't realized that in a few weeks the world he knew would have vanished. When the Allies arrived, one of their first jobs would be to round up the Gestapo. The predators would become the victims.

Nullhausen gave the old man a faint but unmistakable smile. 'I will see what can be done, Mr Tillersland,' he said. 'As I'm sure you appreciate, it depends on the progress of the investigation.'

He stood up and walked to the door. Karl blinked in astonishment as he passed. The gorilla failed to understand that soon the Jersey Gestapo would need as many friends among the islanders as possible.

In the hall a single candle was burning. Nullhausen waited for a moment, trying to locate Marigny. The mutter of voices directed him to a door on the other side of the hall.

He knocked and entered. The room was furnished as a study. It was dominated by a roll-top desk in fumed oak. A large reproduction of Renoir's *Boating Party* was propped against it. Above the desk, where the picture had originally hung, was a recessed wall safe. The door was open.

The other gorilla was working his way along the book-shelves that lined the wall opposite the window. He was pulling out each volume, examining the title, riffling the pages in search of enclosures and dropping it on the floor. To judge by his frowning face, he found the work both absorbing and intellectually demanding. He had a long job in front of him: there were at least a thousand volumes here.

Marigny was leaning on the desk, studying a large book bound in black leather. He glanced up as the door opened.

'It looks good, Kurt,' he said cheerfully. 'Come and see.'

Nullhausen, his face anxious, followed Marigny's pointing finger.

The book was a bible, open at the flyleaf. Like so many bibles, it had been used as a family record.

Augusta Alexandra Tillersland. Born the 23rd of December 1867 and Daughter of the Above; at Bristol; and, in a different hand, below: *Died the 4th of June, 1938, in London. Henry David Howard Tillersland. Born the 20th of July, 1871 and Son of the Above. Married Elizabeth –*

'No, not there,' Marigny said. 'The generation before.'

The ink was more faded and the writing less easy to decipher. *Francis Howard Tillersland. Born the 1st of April, 1832. Married Rachel Leah Goldschmidt, who was baptized into the Christian Faith on the 30th of August, 1865, on the 3rd of September of the same year. God be thanked. Died –*

'Old Henry's a Jewboy,' Marigny said happily. 'With luck we'll find his birth certificate somewhere, and his parents' wedding certificate. Even his mother's birth certificate. But it doesn't matter if we don't: we've got enough to nail him as it is.'

Nullhausen screwed up his face. 'Is it worth it, sir?' he said in an undertone.

Marigny ignored him. 'And not only that, we've found his radio.'

He nodded towards the safe. Nullhausen peered inside. A home-made crystal set, concealed in a tin that had once held Oxo cubes, was on the second shelf down.

'A Jewish subversive,' Marigny said with quiet satisfaction. 'Just as we thought. When we've finished with the house, we'll take them down to headquarters.'

'All of them?'

'All of them.' There was a hint of amusement in Marigny's eyes. 'Any objections, Kurt?'

'No ... no, of course not, sir.' Nullhausen's hands fluttered as if they were pushing away the very possibility that he might object to anything that Marigny chose to say. 'But there is one thing,' he went on, urged both by his own instinct for self-preservation and by the memory of those three shivering people, 'the prisoners are getting very cold. I wondered if you would allow them to get dressed. And perhaps we could all do with a hot drink.'

Marigny pulled out his case and took his time over

27

lighting a cigarette. With narrowed eyes he stared impassively at Nullhausen through the smoke.

'That reminds me,' he said at last, 'we can bring further charges. Hoarding and black-market activities. But you're right: a hot drink would be pleasant. Bring Tillersland in here. You and Karl can take the women to the kitchen. Watch them all the time.'

'And the clothes?'

'Out of the question. We haven't searched the bedrooms yet or checked any of the clothes. We can't take chances. Remember, Kurt: these Jews can be fiendishly cunning. Don't you agree?'

The gorilla threw a particularly heavy volume on the floor, as if lending emphasis to Marigny's question. The noise made Nullhausen jump. Automatically he glanced down at the growing pile of books. Some sort of text-book, he thought; Tillersland had once been an industrial chemist.

'Well?' Marigny prompted him. 'Don't you agree?'

'Yes, sir.' Nullhausen licked his lips and realized that Marigny wanted more than a token assent. 'I – er – I wouldn't trust a Jew farther than I could throw him.'

'Exactly, Kurt. And in that case, I think it would be unwise to take the risk of giving him a drink. Don't you?'

'I wish to telephone my solicitor,' Tillersland said. 'And has the Bailiff been informed that you are holding me?'

He was sitting down, with his hands gripping the seat of the chair. Marigny lounged by the door, his hands deep in the pockets of his coat. They were alone.

The room at headquarters was a long way below ground level. The floor was concrete; the walls were brick and painted regulation beige. The chairs and the table, both of metal painted the same colour, were bolted to the floor.

'My subordinate wishes to torture you,' Marigny said offhandedly. 'Don't be misled by his appearance, by the way. I always think that Karl looks like a moth-eaten teddy bear. But he really is quite *vicious* when roused.'

'You wouldn't be so stupid.'

'Stupid?'

'The islands will be liberated at any moment.'

Marigny nodded slowly. 'It will all be quite chaotic. They are already burning files upstairs.'

There was a spark of anger in the old man's eyes. 'You will have to pay for anything you do to me. Or to Mrs Crozier and Mrs Fishguard.'

'That had occurred to me,' Marigny said drily. 'But has it occurred to you that I may have to pay in any case? Assuming they catch me. You can only pay the same price once.'

'You mean – ?'

'Oh yes. They will call me a war criminal whatever I do to you. Or don't do. So, you see – that consideration is quite irrelevant to our discussion.'

Tillersland passed his hand over his eyes. Fear and tiredness had brought him to the edge of tears.

'Why torture?' he asked. 'I don't deny that the radio is mine. I admit my mother was Jewish. I will plead guilty in court.'

Marigny said nothing.

'It doesn't make sense,' Tillersland muttered. He raised his voice, saying, 'What – what do you *really* want?'

'That's better.' Marigny's lips twitched. 'Such a pleasure to deal with an intelligent man. I'm sure you understand that someone in my position has to make provision against the future. Life is likely to become so – how shall I put it? – precarious, perhaps.' His voice hardened. 'Where have you hidden it?'

'What on earth are you talking about?'

One moment Marigny was leaning against the door, the picture of indolence. A second later he sprang forward and

29

slapped the table with the palm of his hand. Tillersland recoiled.

'The van Gogh, man,' Marigny whispered.

Tillersland looked blankly at him. 'I'm sorry?'

Marigny sighed. 'Let me remind you,' he said softly. '*The Butcher in Les Halles*: your uncle bought it for a few francs in 1887, when he was a student in Paris. He was lucky. No one bought van Gogh in those days. He was *un maudit*, an accursed madman. *The Butcher* is a fascinating picture, too. A transitional work between the Nuenen period and his later Impressionism. It contains the earliest known use of his *bâtonnets* technique. Your uncle died in 1932, and he left it to you.'

Tillersland shrugged. 'You've done your research, I see.'

'You admit you have the picture?'

'"Had" would be more accurate.' Tillersland stared down at the table. 'I sent it to England in April 1940.'

Marigny seized Tillersland's chin between his thumb and forefinger. He tilted the old man's head until their eyes met.

'You are lying again and that is very foolish. You kept the picture in a safe deposit at the St Helier branch of Lloyds Bank. You took it out in May 1940 – I checked the bank's records and I've talked to one of the cashiers. You can have the date and time of day, if you wish.'

'I may have been slightly mistaken about the month. It's a long time ago, you see, and my memory isn't – '

'I have also checked cargo manifests and bills of lading. You sent nothing from Jersey in April or May.'

'A friend took it to London for me. In one of his suitcases. We took it out of the frame and rolled it up.'

Marigny released Tillersland's chin and sat down in the other chair. He took a silk handkerchief from his breast pocket and dabbed his lips. With similarly precise movements – measured to the point of being mannered – he took out his cigarette-case. He chose a cigarette and tapped it on the case.

'I beg your pardon, Mr Tillersland,' he said suddenly. 'What must you think of my manners? A cigarette?'

'I don't smoke, thank you. Not now.'

'Karl's speciality is burning. He prefers cigars, but cigarettes will do. Technique is all – some parts of the anatomy are so much more sensitive than others, don't you agree? Personally, I prefer less obtrusive methods. You can do such a lot with electricity – I'm sure you'll appreciate that, being a scientist yourself. And, of course, a rubber truncheon can leave no external marking if it's applied by an expert. I think we can say that Karl is definitely an expert, if length of experience is anything to go by.'

'There's no point in all this.' Tillersland's voice trembled and Marigny was encouraged. '*The Butcher*'s in London.'

'We have a room next door,' Marigny continued, 'which contains our more sophisticated equipment. Perhaps you would like me to show you round.'

'But I can't tell you – '

'Now be *reasonable*, Mr Tillersland. How can I know that until you've really tried? You cannot blame me for wanting to make sure.'

'It's in London, I swear.'

'I suspect it's still on Jersey. You probably realized it would be safer here, if properly hidden. Less risk of a stray bomb landing on it, eh?'

Marigny strolled over to the door and rapped on it with his knuckles.

'Karl will join us on the guided tour. He won't be a moment.'

The door opened. Marigny slipped outside for a whispered conversation with his colleague. Suddenly both men heard a choking sound in the cell behind them.

Tillersland had half risen from his chair. His face was

31

contorted. He fell sideways, slumped on to the concrete and went into convulsions.

Marigny swore.

A moment later he was kneeling beside the dying man, trying to find the pulse.

Tillersland's hand felt as if it had been refrigerated. His lips were rimmed with froth. The eyes were open; despite the brightness of the overhead light, the pupils were fully dilated. Marigny sniffed and bent closer to Tillersland's face. There was a smell of almonds.

Karl, still standing in the doorway, cleared his throat. 'Is it a heart attack, sir? Shall I get a medic?'

'It's prussic acid, you fool,' Marigny snapped. 'Cyanide.'

A few seconds later, Tillersland died.

PART TWO
NOW –
ANOTHER
SPRING

CHAPTER
3

'You trying to look like a hell's angel or something?'
Detective Chief Inspector Barney Crozier said as he hurried
through the main office. 'I'm sick of it – is that clear?'

'Eh?' Jim Bergerac said. 'Sick of what, Barney?'

'Sick of your scruffy appearance, Sergeant. Where's the
Veldman file?'

'On your desk.'

Crozier stormed into his own office, with Bergerac a few
paces behind him. The Veldman file was exactly where
Bergerac had left it earlier in the afternoon. The only
difference was that now it was partly concealed by a smart,
navy-blue overcoat, which had been tossed on to the desk.
But Crozier failed to see it.

'Well, where the hell is it?'

'Under your coat,' Bergerac said.

Crozier grunted. He scooped up the coat and hung it on
the hook behind the door. As he passed the desk, the flap
of his jacket swept a silver-framed photograph on to the
floor.

Bergerac picked it up. The photograph was several years
old. It showed Barney and Alice Crozier flanking their two
children on a park bench. Everyone was smiling at the
camera, even Barney. Bergerac restored the photograph to
its position on the left of the blotter. Everything on Crozier's
desk had its place.

Crozier sat down in his chair and pointed at one of the
objects in front of him. 'You know what that is?'

Bergerac nodded. 'It looks like your in-tray. With "Pending" below it and the out-tray underneath.'

'Exactly, Sergeant. Very good. And why do we call it an in-tray? Because that's where we put incoming material. You know, memos, letters, files – stuff like that. Like the Veldman file, for example.'

'It was full.'

Crozier ignored this. He opened the file and glanced through it. 'This is going to the Met, you know. I want it word-bloody-perfect.'

'Yes, sir.'

Having failed to find fault with the contents of the file, Crozier reverted to an earlier grievance.

'Why don't you wear a suit more often? I mean, look at you: a grubby old pair of jeans, a beat-up leather jacket – you're not much of an advertisement for the Bureau, are you?'

'I didn't realize we had a dress code – '

'We're dealing with members of the public, Bergerac. Officers should be smartly turned out at all times. Appearances count in this world, even if they don't in the next. You know what you look like? An over-age hooligan. Mutton dressed as lamb.'

'Is there anything else?' Bergerac's voice was still level, but he could feel his temper tugging at its moorings. 'I'm meant to be off duty.'

'So am I,' Crozier said. 'But there's work to do, in case you hadn't noticed.' He glanced up, frowning. 'Oh, go away, will you?'

He flapped the Veldman file in front of him, shooing Bergerac out.

Bergerac began to say something, thought better of it and left the office. On his way out of the Bureau, he stopped by Peggy Masters's desk.

'What's up with Barney?' he asked. 'Have you noticed anything?'

Peggy looked up from her typing. 'He's been rather short with everyone this afternoon. I took him a cup of tea and he was almost offensive about it. Said he'd asked for coffee. I'm *sure* he said tea. And then there's this.' She waved at the paper in the typewriter. 'One tiny mistake and the whole thing has to be done again.'

'Is it important or something?'

'Depends on how you define "important",' Peggy said tartly. 'Personally, I wouldn't have thought a memo to the canteen manager was particularly important. Maybe I'm wrong. Maybe the Chief Inspector's views on the quality of the tuna-fish sandwiches are vital to the Bureau's well-being. But I'm just the secretary. I'm not paid to think.'

'It's unlike him,' Bergerac said.

Peggy's face softened slightly. 'I know he can be a bit hasty, but he's usually fair-minded.' She paused, searching for the right words. 'In fact – for a man – he's not insensitive, when you get to know him.'

Coming from Peggy, that was a compliment. She was not a woman who was lavish with her praise.

'I expect Captain Bligh had a sensitive nature too,' Bergerac said. 'Maybe the mutineers just failed to notice it.'

'This is the Bureau des Etrangers, Jim, not the *Bounty*.'

In another moment, Bergerac thought, she'd be defending her boss with all her might. Crozier didn't deserve her.

'Do you know what's niggling him?' he said. 'We're relatively quiet at present. Has the Committee been shoving its oar in again?'

'Quite the reverse, for once. Charlie Hungerford was here this morning. You know there was a feature in the *Daily Mail* about the Veldman case? He was *so* pleased. There was a lot about the Bureau. They even mentioned the Law and Order Committee, and had a quote from Charlie. "Our police are wonderful" – that sort of thing.'

'So Barney was OK this morning?'

Peggy nodded. 'He was quite cheerful when I went out to lunch.' She glanced up at Bergerac, her eyes bright with intelligence. 'As a matter of fact, I took a call for him just before I left. The Chief Inspector was on the other line, you see. It was Mrs Crozier. She wanted him to phone back as soon as possible.'

'Shoot the bastard, Ricky!'

Bergerac sighed. 'I thought we came here for a quiet drink.'

'I knew those machines were a mistake,' Susan said quietly. 'You know something? This place is doomed.'

They were in Odell's, a small wine bar in Halkett Place, which had opened last winter. At first they had come here just to give it a try because it was new. Later they came because it was conveniently close to the estate agent's where Susan worked and because it never seemed to be crowded. Now they came out of habit. Soon, Bergerac suspected, they wouldn't be coming at all.

The absence of crowds might have been an advantage for Susan Young and Jim Bergerac, but it seemed a little short of disastrous to Robin Odell, the bar's proprietor. Robin had installed the video games in a desperate attempt to attract new customers. The ploy had worked. The only problem was that it attracted the wrong sort of customers.

A burst of muted machine-gun fire filled the bar.

'You blown it, Ricky! You buy the next round.'

'It's the D-Day Landing, I think,' Susan said. 'It's better than the road-hog one with all those horns and squealing tyres.'

Their table was at the other end of the bar from the row of machines. Bergerac had his back to them. He swivelled in his seat. Four youths clustered round one of the games. The nearest table held an impressive collection of empty glasses.

Bergerac glanced at his watch. 'They haven't wasted

time, have they?' He turned back to Susan. 'Want another one?'

'Yes – why not?'

'I can think of one good reason,' Bergerac said.

'They're only kids, Jim.'

Bergerac shrugged. 'There was a fight here on Saturday night. Robin had to call the police. He'll be getting himself a bad name if he's not careful.'

He took their glasses up to the bar. Robin put down the glass he was polishing and asked if they were having the same again. He was a paunchy man in early middle age with a lugubrious face, which seemed to grow a little sadder with every passing day.

'It was a good move, getting those machines,' he said glumly as he measured out Susan's gin. 'Don't you agree?'

'Not really,' Bergerac said. 'Are they making your fortune?'

'Well, not exactly. More like keeping the overdraft from getting worse.' Odell reached for the tonic water. 'The problem is, the other profits have dropped since I installed them. There just doesn't seem to be the same demand for bar snacks and the more up-market wines.'

'Swings and roundabouts?'

'Something like that.' Robin nodded in a worldly-wise manner. 'Of course, seasonal fluctuations are only to be expected in this business.' He opened the ice bucket and his face became a few degrees more mournful. 'Damn, I'll have to get some more ice.'

He vanished beneath the marble-topped counter. It sounded as though he were chipping the ice out with a pickaxe.

'Trade will pick up in the summer,' he went on. 'After all, it isn't even Easter yet.'

Bergerac privately doubted that Odell's would still be open in the summer. Robin had left a secure job as a computer programmer to start this place; he knew a little about wine and nothing about business; he had his savings, a bank loan and a wholly romanticized view of the joys of self-employment in the licensed trade. On the one and only occasion that Diamanté Lil had visited the wine bar, she had summed its chances up in one sentence: 'This place has the kiss of death on it.'

Odell poured out Bergerac's St Clements and took the money. While he was at the till, one of the young men staggered over to the bar. He slammed the metal tray on the counter.

'Four pints of Foster's, mate. And look sharp.'

Bergerac looked him up and down, without making his interest too obvious. The newcomer was burly, dark haired and unshaven. He wore an oil-stained denim jacket, which had been decorated inexpertly with leather patches and metal studs. It was just the sort of jacket that Barney Crozier would appreciate. Bergerac's lips twitched with amusement.

'What you grinning at, then?'

'I was admiring your jacket,' Bergerac said. 'You do it yourself? *Very* talented.'

The young man blinked, uncertain whether to take the remark as genuine or sarcastic. He decided to play it safe.

'What's it to you?' he snarled. He swayed a few inches closer and knocked over one of the glasses.

'Nothing, chum,' Bergerac said gently. Odell handed him his change. 'Thanks, Robin.'

He turned his back on the youth and carried the drinks over to Susan.

She sipped her gin. 'Living dangerously again?' she murmured.

'I meant it,' Bergerac said. 'It's just the sort of jacket I need for work.'

But Susan wasn't listening. 'I know one of those kids. The small one. At least, I've met him somewhere.'

Bergerac looked over his shoulder. Robin was still serving

the proud possessor of the customized denim jacket. Of the remaining three, two of them were refighting D-Day; the third, the smallest of the quartet, was leaning against a table and rolling a cigarette. As Bergerac watched, the tobacco slid out of the paper and cascaded to the floor.

The boy swore, glancing round to see if his companions had noticed his lack of expertise. There was something pathetic in the gesture, for it implied a craving for their approval as well as a fear of their ridicule. For the first time Bergerac saw his face.

Susan gave the ghost of a chuckle. 'There's nothing quite so unmacho as failing to roll a cigarette. He really should practise in private.'

Brown eyes; dark, expensively cut hair; a pale complexion; and features that might one day be handsome, once the face had lost the gawkiness and spots of adolescence.

Bergerac had seen a younger version of that face earlier today. Then the face had been smiling; now it looked as though its owner were in training for the title role in *Hamlet*.

'What is it, Jim?'

He turned back to her. 'That's Richard Crozier, Barney's son. You probably remember his face from the Bureau's Christmas party.'

'He's never *Barney*'s son, is he? That tearaway? I'm sure he didn't look like that when I saw him.'

'I expect Barney and Alice had him dry-cleaned beforehand,' Bergerac said absently. 'Susan, he shouldn't be here. He's only about fifteen, I think – even younger than Kim.'

'He looks older, to give him his due.'

'Robin should have more sense. And there'll be hell to pay if this gets out.'

'For Richard?'

'And for Robin. And maybe for Barney too if the papers get hold of it. You can see it now. BUREAU CHIEF'S SON IN UNDER-AGE DRINKING SPREE. And it won't do Alice much good, either.'

41

'What are you going to do?'

A chair fell over with a clatter as Denim Jacket took the drinks over to his friends. Bergerac looked round again. He was just in time to see Richard Crozier opening the door marked 'Toilets'.

He patted Susan's hand. 'I think I'll go to the loo.'

Above the urinal stretched a tempting expanse of white tiles.

A number of people had already succumbed to temptation. Broadly speaking, the creative spirits fell into one of two categories, the intelligentsia and *vox populi*.

The intelligentsia were motivated by a simple desire to show off their intelligence.

> *Shakespeare: To be or not to be.*
> *Sartre: To be is to do.*
> *Sinatra: Do be do be do.*

My inferiority complexes aren't as good as yours.

Or, more ambitiously, a limerick that began:

> *There was a young man in St Helier,*
> *Who lived in an artist's atelier*

The next two lines of the limerick were obscene. The fifth petered out for want of another rhyme for St Helier.

Vox populi, on the other hand, wanted merely to communicate some overriding emotion, and usually its graffiti were models of clarity and brevity. There was nothing ambiguous about *Up Manchester United*. The main topics were sport, sex and the Jersey States Police.

Richard Crozier studied the graffiti with difficulty; he was swaying so much that he had to prop himself up with his free hand. He zipped himself up just as the lavatory door opened.

Richard pulled out a felt-tip pen. He assumed the new arrival was Dave or Steve or Tom.

'How about this as a definition for a copper?' he said as he wrote. 'What do you call a castrated pig – disgruntled?'

No reply; no approaching footsteps. The silence made him turn his head.

A man in a leather jacket was leaning, arms folded across the chest, against the door.

Richard felt himself flushing. He capped the felt-tip.

'Mr Bergerac! I . . .'

'If I went in for graffiti, I'd try and avoid cheap remarks about my father's job. After all, it paid for things like the fancy haircut, didn't it?'

The flush deepened into an ugly red stain. 'That's my business.' Richard hesitated and, when Bergerac said nothing in return, gathered courage from the silence. 'Why don't you get off my back? You spying on me or something?'

His voice came out as a croak, which didn't help his self-esteem.

Bergerac sighed. 'I can do this two ways, Richard. I can tell Odell you're an under-age drinker and watch him chucking you out. Or I can go back in there and finish my drink – and watch you leave of your own free will.'

'I'm not a bloody child – '

'I know you're not. That's why I'm giving you a choice.'

'Ah, piss off,' Richard muttered.

Bergerac appeared not to have heard. Richard wondered what would happen if he appealed to the others for support. The trouble was, Bergerac was blocking the door.

'You make me sick,' Richard said. 'All of you. Bloody spies – what's it to you how I spend my time?'

He took a couple of steps towards the door and staggered into the wash-basin. The walls were rocking. Suddenly fresh air seemed the most desirable thing in the world.

'As a matter of fact,' he said, slurring the words together, 'I was just going.'

Bergerac moved away from the door. 'After you,' he said.

CHAPTER
4

With his usual anxiety, the taxi-driver watched the foot
passengers coming along Albert Pier.

The Portsmouth ferry was on time this evening. It wasn't
even eight o'clock. Just the one fare, he promised himself,
and then he'd go home to supper. With luck he'd be home
by 8.30. Might even see something of the kids tonight.
Maybe that wasn't such a good idea after all. The kids
weren't exactly restful.

He scanned the approaching passengers with an experienced eye. In this job, you had to be selective. You didn't
want the drunks who had spent the nine-hour crossing
tanking up in the bar; you didn't want the young couples
with hordes of screaming kids who left chewing gum on the
upholstery; and you didn't want the elderly people with
eighty-five suitcases, all heavier than themselves, which
they expected someone else to carry for them.

In the rear-view mirror he saw two passengers peel away
from the column and head towards him. A youngish man
in dark glasses held the arm of an old woman who was
carrying a white cane; their only luggage seemed to be one
medium-sized suitcase. It was difficult to see much of the
man's face, partly because of the glasses and partly because
he was wearing a trench coat with the collar turned up
against the cold. The taxi-driver's anxiety vanished. He
rolled down his window.

'We want the Hôtel de Bretagne,' the man said. He had
one of those resonant voices that make the words they say
seem much more important than they are. 'Is that far?'

The driver shook his head. 'Half a mile or so. Nothing's far on this island.' He swivelled in his seat and opened the offside rear door for them. 'Do you want me to put the case in the boot?'

'No need,' the man said. 'Plenty of room in the back.'

He helped the old lady into the car with a solicitousness that won the driver's approval. It was nice to see a bloke being kind to his old mum. The man went round to the other side of the car and opened the nearside door. There was enough space for their legs and the suitcase in the well between the seats. If they tipped generously and didn't smoke on the journey, these two would be damn near perfect.

'Nice hotel, the Bretagne.' The driver believed that chatting cost nothing and could be good for tips. 'Been there before?'

'No,' the man said. 'This is our first visit to the island.'

'I bet it won't be your last.' He eased the cab into the traffic. 'People tend to come back, you know. You tourists?'

'That's right,' the man agreed. 'Just tourists.'

His voice didn't encourage further conversation. The old woman said nothing at all. During the journey she stared out of the window. The driver wondered if she was still partially sighted, despite the cane. Maybe the bloke's eyes weren't too good either and that was why he was wearing dark glasses; these things could be hereditary.

While they were waiting for a traffic-light to change, he caught sight of the woman's face in the mirror. The light from a street lamp had turned it an unhealthy shade of yellow. But that was not the reason why his hands tightened on the steering wheel.

My God – he must be imagining things.

The features were twisted with hatred. The lips moved but no sounds emerged. She looked totally off her head.

He blinked and looked again.

The old lady was smiling now as she looked out of the

window. She looked like everyone's old granny. As sweet as apple pie.

'This is all new,' the woman said as the rear lights of the taxi disappeared down the curving drive of the Hôtel de Bretagne. 'The island even *smells* different.'

'Well, what do you expect?' the man said impatiently. 'Things change in forty years. Come on.'

'I hope some things haven't changed.'

'So do I – for both our sakes.'

He took her arm and led her into the foyer. The doorman, seeing the suitcase, automatically pointed them in the direction of reception. A heavily made-up young woman looked up from the accounts she was checking. Her smile was designed to be welcoming, but she had smiled it so often at complete strangers that it no longer had any real warmth.

'Mr Winston Arkwright,' the man said. 'I made a telephone booking yesterday – two single rooms.'

'Oh, yes.' She ran her pen down a computer print-out and ticked one of the entries. 'You're in 423, sir, and Mrs Arkwright's next door in 424. Just bed and breakfast, isn't it?'

Mr Arkwright nodded.

She pushed the registration forms towards him. 'If you'd just sign here.' While he was writing, she summoned the duty-porter and handed him the keys. 'Will you be wanting dinner, sir? I believe there's still room in the restaurant.'

Arkwright shook his head. 'My mother's tired. We'll have a sandwich from room service.'

He turned to go, still holding the old woman's arm. Suddenly he stopped – so abruptly that his mother cannoned into him.

'Are there telephone directories in the rooms?' he demanded.

'Of course, sir – for Jersey, that is. You just dial o for an outside line. If you – '

Arkwright cut her off in mid-sentence by moving away. He towed his mother towards the lifts. The porter shrugged at the receptionist – the phrase 'thank you' wasn't in the vocabulary of some of the Bretagne's guests – and followed in their wake.

'Tonight?' he heard the old woman say.

'Why not?' Arkwright said. 'The sooner the better.'

'One round of ham sandwiches,' Mrs Arkwright said, 'and I'll have the smoked salmon with salad. No, half a bottle of Veuve Clicquot. With a pot of coffee for two, OK? Yes, room 424.'

She put the phone down. Arkwright looked up from the telephone directory.

'Smoked salmon?' he said. 'Veuve Clicquot? Pushing the boat out, aren't you?'

Her lips tightened. 'I've waited long enough for this.'

'I still think we should find somewhere cheaper in the morning.'

She shook her head vigorously. 'It's ideal, Winston – big and anonymous. Besides, I want to pamper myself for a while.'

'There'll be time for that later.'

'Well, I want it now, do you hear?' Her voice began to rise. 'It's my savings we're using – remember that. I'll do as I damned well please.'

'All right, Mother.' Arkwright's eyes, though no longer masked by the dark glasses, were expressionless. He tapped the open page of the directory. 'I've found your friend George, by the way.'

The anger faded from her face. 'What's the address?'

'8 Woodbridge House, Coleford Road, St Helier. I presume it's a block of flats. Mean anything to you?'

'Coleford Road does. It's somewhere off Queen's Road. A turning on the right, I think. Is the son in there too?'

'Barney? I think so – there's a "Crozier, B & A" in Beaumont. He's married, isn't he? Must be him.'

There was a knock on the door. 'Room service.'

'One moment.' Arkwright closed the directory and slipped on his glasses. 'But I hope we won't have to bother him.'

'I don't know.' Mrs Arkwright spoke too softly for her son to hear. She rocked to and fro in her chair, hugging herself. 'If he's anything like his mother, I'd love to bother him.'

Like priests and doctors, a policeman is never entirely off duty.

Bergerac was driving through a side-road in the outskirts of St Helier when he noticed the four youths clustered outside the lighted window of a small off-licence. He was on his way back from visiting a retired Anglican clergyman in Gorey. The clergyman, another member of Alcoholics Anonymous, had been going through a rough patch lately. Bergerac had spent the evening with him; it had been more of a pleasure than a chore, since over the years an unlikely but firm friendship had developed between the two of them.

The youths were doing nothing obviously wrong. But good coppers notice people automatically, with the same sixth sense that farmers use when they feel a change in the weather.

He saw them no longer than a couple of seconds, but that was enough to remind him he was a policeman. It was something to do with the way they were huddled together, with their shoulders hunched, and something to do with the way in which one of them glanced swiftly up the otherwise deserted road when he heard the Triumph's engine. None of them wanted his face to be seen. The fact that the window belonged to an off-licence was another pointer. The street lamp beside the shop was out of action.

Even so, it was almost certainly nothing to do with him. Besides, he was late already – he was meant to be collecting Susan from a friend's house, where she was having dinner. Bergerac's lack of punctuality was a constant bone of contention between them.

But his reflexes took control of his actions. He signalled a left turn. In a couple of minutes he had fetched a compass and was approaching the off-licence again from the same direction as before.

Bergerac changed down to second and switched the headlights on to full beam.

The four youths, still facing the window, were trapped in the glare. Two of them were carrying bricks.

Bergerac never knew what to say in situations like this. It always sounded like a cliché, even if you didn't sink to the depth of 'What's all this, then?'

Rolling down the window, he braked and pulled in at the kerb.

'And what are you doing?' he said. 'Bricklaying at night school?'

It would have been all right if the tallest of the bunch hadn't panicked. He swung round and threw his brick at Bergerac's head.

His aim was as poor as his intelligence. The brick missed the open window and crashed into the door itself.

Before that, Bergerac had merely been doing his duty. He didn't want to arrest anyone; prevention was better than cure.

Now, however, both duty and inclination propelled him out of the car. Damage to property was an offence – but a wanton attack on his beloved Triumph Roadster was a personal injury.

Angry though he was, Bergerac's mind was working

coolly. There were four of them, and one of them still had a brick. Not the best of odds.

'Run, Sean!' one of them said.

Instead, Sean launched himself at Bergerac.

Bergerac grabbed the oncoming fist with both hands, bent his knees and swung the youth over his shoulder. Sean, completely out of control, bounced off the bonnet of the Triumph and rolled into the gutter. One of the remaining youths dropped his brick, darted across the road and disappeared into a narrow alley. His heavy boots clattered on the asphalt. The second followed him almost immediately.

Only the fourth was left, and he was the smallest of the lot. The odds had shortened to two to one.

Sean tried to scramble to his feet. Bergerac pushed him back to the ground. Out of the corner of his eye, he saw a blur of movement. He was too late to do anything.

A pair of arms wrapped themselves round his knees in a classic rugby tackle. He fell to the pavement, with his assailant on top of him. They thrashed clumsily and painfully on the unyielding surface, trying to get a grip on one another.

It was a foregone conclusion – if Sean didn't intervene. Bergerac was older, heavier, wilier and a lot more experienced. A few seconds later he had the youth in a headlock.

Both of them were gasping for breath. The youth was almost sobbing with rage or fear. Apart from that, all Bergerac could hear was the sound of running footsteps. He was not altogether surprised that Sean had decided that discretion was the better part of valour.

He pulled his prisoner towards the headlights. 'You really are a fool, aren't you?' he said. 'All those heroics, and they go and leave you in the lurch.'

The first thing he saw was that there was an ugly graze on the boy's cheekbone; that's what came of rolling around on pavements with strange policemen.

'There's a moral here, you know. If — '

Bergerac stopped abruptly as the pale features reassembled themselves into a face.

He had just collared Richard Crozier.

CHAPTER
5

Winston Arkwright was still thinking about his mother as he turned into Coleford Road.

As he was leaving, she had been on the phone to room service, ordering another half-bottle of champagne. She had drunk the first bottle, with her little finger genteelly crooked, in about ten minutes. He was furious with her and her self-indulgence. When she was tipsy, she couldn't keep her mouth shut. The old bitch would ruin everything if he didn't watch out.

But he couldn't afford an open quarrel with her − not yet. That was the main reason why he had decided to make a reconnaissance now, rather than wait until the morning. If he had stayed in the hotel bedroom with her any longer, he knew he would have lost his temper. He always lost his temper if he was alone with his mother for any length of time. The nine-hour crossing to St Helier had been sheer torture.

Coleford Road was a winding cul-de-sac, which crawled up the side of a hill. A fine drizzle was falling. Arkwright was wearing a flat tweed cap as well as the mackintosh that looked like a trench coat. But he had discarded the dark glasses. It was ridiculous of his mother to insist on them. They made him far too conspicuous. Originally she had wanted him to grow a beard, but he had drawn the line at that. He would need a much better reason than she could supply before he agreed to ruin his profile. Damn it, his face was his fortune. Her fear that someone would recognize it was absurd. She might live in the past, but no one else did.

On one side of the road was a line of semi-detached houses, probably about fifty years old. Opposite them, the buildings were more varied. He passed several houses that stood back in their own grounds, a Methodist chapel, three modern bungalows, a block of purpose-built flats and a small park with swings and slides. A nice residential area, he thought with a sneer. Not affluent but comfortable.

Woodbridge House was beyond the litle park. It was screened from the road by a row of dripping limes, which were probably older than the flats themselves. Arkwright peered up the path that led to the communal front door.

It was another purpose-built block, smaller and more modern than the last one he had passed. This one was an ugly, jerry-built job – typical post-war rubbish. There were lights in some of the windows, though the top floor was entirely in darkness.

Arkwright, whose tastes (if not his purse) ran to eight-eenth-century town houses in gracious squares, despised the flats and their occupants. How could anyone *choose* to live in such an aesthetically unappealing building? If his mother was right, George Crozier should have been able to afford something a good deal better.

By now it was raining harder. He pushed open the gate and made a cautious circuit of the building. To one side was a driveway, which led to eight prefabricated garages at the back. He glanced upwards and established that the top-floor rooms on this side were in darkness too.

A shadow crossed a window on the second storey. Hastily he moved on. He negotiated a line of dustbins and passed through an archway. Here, on the other side of the block and dimly illuminated by the street-lighting, that filtered through the bare branches of the limes, was a small, untidy garden, presumably for the use of residents.

He was back at the gate. There was no point in doing anything tonight. These things had to be planned. Then he hesitated. It might be worth checking that Crozier still

lived here. He had found the address in last year's telephone directory. The old man might have moved in the
meantime. Arkwright plodded through the rain to the front
door. If he wasn't careful, these shoes would be ruined.

There were eight buzzers on the left of the door. The top
one had Crozier's name against it. Above the buzzers was
the grill for the intercom. It was a pity that the main door
was locked. Still, one could usually find a way round these
little difficulties.

Suddenly the door opened from the inside. Arkwright,
whose attention was still concentrated on the buzzers, was
taken completely by surprise. Fortunately, the man coming
out was looking over his shoulder.

'See you tomorrow, then,' he called out.

A woman's voice floated down the stairs. 'Drive carefully,
Frank.'

Chuckling, Frank surged through the doorway without
looking where he was going. He barged into Arkwright on
the doorstep.

'Sorry, mate.'

'Er – not at all.'

A wave of gin and tobacco enveloped Arkwright. Frank
glanced incuriously at him.

'God, it's pissing cats and dogs! You going in?'

'Oh . . .' Arkwright put his hand on the open door. Frank
ran clumsily down the path, sheltering his head with a
newspaper. 'Thank you,' Arkwright called after him.
'Good-night.'

It was a gift from the gods. Arkwright had long since
learned the wisdom of accepting divine largess when it was
offered. He slipped into the hall. He just had time to see
two doors one on either side of him, and a staircase in front
of him.

Then the lights went out.

The darkness hit him like a blow. For an instant he was
on the verge of panic. A door closed, somewhere above his

head. He stiffened, waiting for the sound of footsteps approaching on the stairs.

Nothing but silence. It must have been Frank's friend closing her front door. Simultaneously he realized that there was probably a time-switch controlling the lights. He ran his hand along the wall by the door until he found it. When the light came on again, he discovered that his hands were clammy with sweat.

The flash of panic shamed him. For the sake of his self-respect, he wanted to do something that showed he wasn't afraid.

He studied the hallway. The flats on either side were numbered one and two. It was a four-storey building. Crozier's flat was almost certainly on the top floor.

Judging by the absence of lighted windows, the old man was either asleep or out. There was an easy way to find out.

Arkwright opened the front door again. He stood in the porch, keeping the door open with his foot, and pressed the top buzzer three times. He waited and tried again.

There was no answer – as he had both hoped and feared. *What now? Attack or retreat?*

The hall light went out again. He cursed under his breath.

He switched it on. The memory of that shameful panic made up his mind for him. If you once gave in to fear, you could spend your life being afraid. He closed the door gently behind him.

Then he began to climb the stairs.

'Oh don't bother, Barney,' George Crozier said. 'It's a filthy night. I'll ring for a taxi.'

'No, you won't,' his son said. 'It won't take a moment to run you home. Anyway, the car's in the drive still.'

'I don't like to be a burden.'

'You're not, Dad. I want to put the car in the garage.'

Alice Crozier stood up. 'I'll get your coat.' She never knew what to call her father-in-law, so usually she didn't give him any name at all.

On her way to the door she passed the sideboard. She glanced at the whisky bottle. The old reprobate had put away nearly a third of a bottle of Johnny Walker Black Label this evening. It was a disgusting example to set the children. Not that they were here tonight – Clare was upstairs asleep and Richard was out somewhere.

To give him his due, George didn't act as if he were drunk. He seemed to have an infinite capacity for alcohol. In a way that made him an even worse example for the children to follow.

When she got back into the room, both men were on their feet. George was in the act of relighting the blackened briar that accompanied him everywhere he went. Alice would not have been surprised to learn that he smoked it in bed and in the bath.

'Thanks for supper, Alice.' George pecked her on the cheek. 'I always say you're a smashing cook.'

The remark immediately made her wonder what else he said about her. 'Supper' grated on her, too – she wished he would learn that they called the evening meal 'dinner' in this house.

'Won't be long, love,' Barney said as they left. 'Don't wait up.'

Of course she would wait up. Richard wasn't back yet.

As a dutiful daughter-in-law should, she stood in the doorway to wave them off. Then she went quietly upstairs.

There was always the hope that he had slipped into the house without them hearing. It was just possible, she told herself. Her heart leapt when she noticed the line of light around his door.

Her daughter's light was off. Alice paused outside the open door until the sound of Clare's regular breathing had reassured her. Then she tapped lightly on Richard's door.

There was no answer. Of course there wasn't any answer. She had allowed hope to fool her again.

She pushed the door open and stuck her head into the room. The bedside lamp was on, shedding a puddle of light on the unmade bed. As usual, the bedroom looked as though a typhoon had made a flying visit. You couldn't even see the carpet for the layer of discarded clothes, books and record sleeves.

Kids had it so damned easy, these days. She glanced round the room. The portable television and the music centre were like personal insults; she had thought herself lucky to have a second-hand transistor radio. The walls were covered with posters and paintings: the posters were mainly of garishly unappetizing pop stars; the paintings, most of which were by Richard himself, were even more unsettling – he spent far too much time fiddling around with paintbrushes.

Maybe it would have been better if they could have afforded to send him to a public school. But there just hadn't been the money. They could have managed it if George had sold the cottage and shared the proceeds with them, as he had talked of doing just after Marie Crozier died. The cottage wasn't any use to him. After all, it would come to Barney sooner or later.

On top of the chest of drawers was an exercise book from school. The cover had been decorated with a swirl of bilious colours, among which it was just possible to discern the word 'PRIVATE'. Alice had strong views about respecting the privacy of children. But, before she knew what she was doing, she had opened the book.

March 19. The trouble with my parents is that they –

She heard a car in the road. For an instant she thought it was Barney. Guilt infected her with urgency: she slammed the book shut and went out on to the landing.

Of course, it wasn't Barney. It was far too soon for him to be back. With a massive effort of will she forced herself not to go back into Richard's room. She was trembling. Some things it was better not to know.

But where the hell is he this time?

Her teeth dug into her lower lip. If she wasn't careful, she was going to cry.

'Richard's OK, isn't he?'

Barney Crozier frowned. Sometimes his father had an uncanny knack of echoing his own thoughts. Or maybe it was the other way round.

The wipers were going at full speed, but still the windscreen was a blur of running water. Traffic-lights were coming up. He changed down.

'Yes, he's fine.'

'Out with friends tonight?'

'That's right.' He braked and stopped. 'God knows where, though. I don't.' His father's silence made him continue. He added, half in explanation, 'It worries his mother.'

'Like you worried yours.'

'Come off it, Dad. We were all pretty innocent then. Not like kids today.'

'That's not the point.' The old man's tone was tart. 'These things are relative.'

The lights changed to green. Crozier turned left into Elizabeth Place.

'It's like he's turned into someone else over the last few months,' he said. 'His school reports are awful. Today he didn't even bother to turn up – the school had to ring Alice at work. He's never at home if he can help it. And when he is, all he does is watch TV or listen to that bloody music at full volume. Music! That's a joke.'

'What about his painting?' George said. 'Still doing that?'

Barney snorted. 'For what it's worth, yes. Says he wants to go to art college.'

'Well, why not?'

59

'Because it'll get him nowhere in the long run. If he had any sense he'd concentrate on science subjects. That's where the demand is. Besides, he isn't even any good. Anyone with half an eye can see that.'

George relit his pipe. Barney glanced at him and felt the familiar blend of affection and exasperation. His car was a non-smoking area. For everyone except George.

'Your mother used to paint a bit,' the old man said.

'Did she? I never knew that.'

'It was before the war, mainly – when we were courting and just after we were married. Little watercolours, nothing fancy. She liked painting people's faces.'

'Any good?'

'I liked them. She always said they were terrible.' George sniffed. 'I don't know much about art myself, but old Tillersland thought they were good. He knew a lot about pictures.'

'So why did she stop?'

'During the war she didn't get much chance to do anything. And afterwards you came along: there wasn't any time and she sort of lost the habit.'

Barney, startled by this new sidelight on his mother, braked too sharply at the next lights.

'Have you got any of her pictures?' he asked. 'Why haven't I seen them before?'

George's pipe had acquired a blockage. He sucked furiously at it but failed to clear the stem. He stuffed the pipe in his pocket.

'I thought you wouldn't be interested. She lost heart after Tillersland died. Really cut her up, that did. She threw out most of the paintings when I came back from the war and she moved out of Wellington Road. I kept a few – you can see them if you want. They're in that box I gave you, along with those old photos and her letters.'

'I've never looked in there.'

A silence stretched between them. George had given

Barney the box a couple of years ago, just after Marie Crozier's death. *You might as well have this now. It's family stuff – might interest you one day.* Barney had helped George clear out the house where his parents had lived for nearly thirty years. It had been a depressing business for both of them.

George had sold a few things, thrown out a lot and given the remainder to Barney and Alice. As he had said, he didn't need much in that little flat.

For some reason, Barney Crozier had never wanted to open the dented, japanned box, not while George was alive. It belonged to his father. It was private.

George cleared his throat. 'Well – have a look sometime. Not the letters, maybe – not yet. See what Richard thinks of the paintings. He'd probably laugh his head off.'

They were in Queen's Road now. Not far to go. Barney wasn't sure if he was glad or sorry.

The old man pressed on relentlessly. 'Your mother was always sorry that you showed no inclinations that way.'

'What – for painting?'

George nodded.

Barney Crozier's laugh was closer to a bark. 'Talk about parents wanting their kids to live out their own fantasies.'

'Yes,' his father said. 'That's exactly what I was thinking. It makes it tough for the kids, doesn't it?'

It took Barney a few seconds to realize that his father wasn't just admitting his own mistakes. He was also warning Barney not to repeat them with Richard.

I must be mad.

The four words ran round Arkwright's head like a refrain as he moved methodically through the flat. The lock had been child's play to someone with his skills. He left the front door ajar. Sound travelled well up the uncarpeted stairs. He should have enough warning if Crozier came back. He could hide in the alcove on the landing outside.

61

Nevertheless, he was terrified. Only the unreality of the situation kept him from an inglorious retreat.

I must be mad.

Luckily, the flat was small. The front door gave on to a minute hall. There were four doors – to the sitting-room, the one bedroom, the kitchen and the bathroom. Arkwright drew the curtains. The fabric was thick and heavy, but he dared not turn on the lights. He made do with his torch.

The place was very tidy and clean. George Crozier seemed to have few possessions – and none of them were worth nicking in themselves. The flat was comfortable, but there were no obvious signs of wealth. Arkwright wondered if his mother had overestimated the size of the inheritance.

He tried the obvious places first: the drawers in the ornate Edwardian sideboard that dwarfed the sitting-room; the shelves in the wardrobe; the battered mahogany writing-case on top of the bookshelves. In all of them he drew a blank. There were few memorabilia of any description, apart from the wedding photograph in the bedroom. It was all so damned impersonal.

He broadened his search but met with no more success. In the end he was reduced to pulling out the books to see if anything had been hidden behind them. Nothing was. It was infuriating that he should have made all this effort to no purpose. It was unfair.

He glanced automatically at the titles of some of the books. *A Plain Man's Guide to Socialism* rubbed shoulders with Koestler's *The Roots of Coincidence*. Volumes from the Left Book Club mingled with bright new paperbacks about aspects of the occult.

Socialism and the paranormal? An odd pair of interests. It looked as if old Crozier was a bit of a crank.

A door closed, somewhere far below him.

Arkwright jumped like a startled rabbit. He darted towards the door to the hall, colliding with a small table on the way. He picked it up, but as he bent down the cuff of his coat swept a magazine from the arm of a chair. Replacing it cost him more precious seconds. His cap fell off; he stuffed it in his pocket.

At last he was out on the landing. The footsteps were coming closer. They had reached the floor below. Arkwright closed the door silently behind him. No time to try to relock it.

No time at all.

The old man came round the bend in the stairs. Arkwright skipped away from the door. It must be George Crozier – this little fellow with the red cheeks.

'Hello!' the old man said. 'Looking for me?'

'No.' Arkwright waved vaguely at the other door. 'Number 7, actually.'

He smiled and started down the stairs, hoping that the trembling in his legs wasn't visible. It was vital that he should act naturally. *The performance of my life – before an audience of one.*

A naked light bulb dangled above the stairwell. Arkwright suddenly realized that his cap was still in his pocket. *I must be mad.* He felt terribly exposed.

The old man frowned as they came level. 'Don't I know you, son?'

'No, I don't think we've met.' Arkwright slid past him. 'Ah – good-night.'

'Could have sworn I'd seen your face somewhere.' Crozier shrugged and continued on his way. 'Good-night.'

Arkwright walked steadily down the first flight of stairs. He heard the rattle of keys above his head.

On the next flight he began to run.

CHAPTER
6

'Over there,' Bergerac said.

Richard Crozier zigzagged across the living-room. The pallor of his face had acquired an ominous tinge of green. He tried to open the cupboard where the coats were kept.

'No,' Bergerac said patiently. 'The other door.'

Richard staggered into the bathroom. He retained enough presence of mind to kick the door shut behind him. Thirty seconds later the retching began. Bergerac hoped the boy's aim was good.

He put the kettle on and measured twice the normal quantity of coffee into the jug. He poured a pint glass of mineral water and found the aspirins. The old routine gave him a certain nostalgic pleasure.

The lavatory flushed, but the bathroom door remained closed.

Bergerac found the telephone number of Susan's friend, rang it and asked to speak to Susan.

She came on the line almost immediately. 'You're late, Jim.'

'I'm sorry – something's come up.'

'So when can I expect you?'

'I'm not sure. Look, can you get a taxi home? I'm at my flat at present. I'll come over as soon as I can.'

'Constabulary duty, eh?'

'Something like that.' The lavatory flushed again. 'Susan, I must go. I really am sorry, OK?'

'I'll take your apologies in person,' she said. 'Actions speak louder than words, remember? Take care.'

As he put down the phone, the bathroom door opened. Richard's face was still pale, but the hint of green had gone. Bergerac pointed him towards an armchair. The boy reached it more or less in a straight line. If nothing else, Bergerac thought, the young were enviably resilient.

Richard slumped into the chair. Bergerac put the water and the aspirins beside him.

'I'd take three of those, if I were you,' he said. 'For starters. And we'd better do something about your face.'

The boy shook his head feebly and then groaned.

Bergerac turned away to make the coffee. Behind him he heard the rattle of aspirin. While the coffee was brewing, he went into the bathroom. Richard had made a commendable effort to clear up after him. Bergerac found the plasters and the disinfectant in the medicine cabinet. He opened the window to clear the smell. Before he went back to the living-room, he slipped into the bedroom to fetch the cotton wool which Susan used for her make-up.

Richard accepted the black coffee with a nod that might have been his way of saying 'thank you'. He sipped it and pulled a face.

'Drink it up,' Bergerac said. 'It'll do you good.'

'Where am I?' the boy demanded suddenly. His colour was better, but his voice was still slurred.

'This is my flat.'

'But why are we here? Why not the station?'

Bergerac raised his eyebrows. 'You'd *rather* be there?'

'It's where you take people when you arrest them.' Richard's bravado was obviously ebbing, but he plunged on. 'Why should I be any different?'

'Who said you'd been arrested?'

The boy covered his confusion by having another sip of coffee. His face was sullen.

'Oh, I get it,' he said at last. 'Dad's your boss, isn't he? You don't have the guts to nick the boss's son.'

Bergerac grinned.

'Well? Am I right?'

'No. You're just about as wrong as you can be.' Bergerac hesitated. 'If you want to do this formally, we can. Drunk and disorderly. Assaulting a police officer. Damage to property. It won't be much fun for you – but that's your affair. But it does seem a bit rough on your parents.'

'It's my life. I'll do what I want.'

Bergerac shrugged. 'Who's stopping you? If you want to play martyrs, go ahead. The press will get hold of it, of course.'

'Who cares?'

'Your parents will. I don't just mean because of *you*. I'm talking about the damage it could do to *their* careers, not to yours.'

Richard stared silently at his coffee. He was blushing again.

Bergerac swiftly changed the subject before the silence could get any more awkward than it already was. 'We'd better clean up that graze of yours,' he said. 'Here.' He tossed the packet of plasters on to Richard's lap. 'Can you get one out? One of the smaller ones should do.'

He poured TCP on a piece of cotton wool and swabbed Richard's cheek. It could have been much worse: the cut, which was along the line of the cheekbone, was small and shallow. The area around it was already coming up in a bruise. Richard winced as the disinfectant bit into the graze. Bergerac covered the cut with a plaster.

The boy cleared his throat. 'I . . . I'm sorry about your car.'

'You didn't chuck the brick.'

'Is it badly damaged?'

Bergerac shook his head. 'It wasn't dented, thank God. Nothing a lick of paint can't handle.'

Richard finished his coffee. 'If you want, I'll help you do it.'

'Thanks. I might take you up on that. You any good with a paintbrush?'

For the first time the boy's eyes met Bergerac's. 'That's one thing I can do,' he said, unconsciously arrogant. 'Paint, I mean.'

'Well, that's something. When I try and paint, I get it everywhere except the right place.'

'It's probably because you put too much on the brush.' The confidence evaporated as suddenly as it had come. 'What happens now?'

'You have another mug of coffee and I drive you home.'

'You going to tell my father?'

'I wasn't planning to.'

'Why not?'

Bergerac hesitated. 'Let's just say I don't think it would serve any useful purpose. Unless you're intending to carry on the way you were this evening.'

Richard said nothing.

'Those mates of yours,' Bergerac went on, 'they're trouble. I suppose that's part of their charm. But remember what they did tonight: ran off and left you to carry the can.'

'I'm not making any promises,' Richard said. 'My friends are my affair.'

The words were braver than his face.

'I'm not asking for promises.' Bergerac refilled Richard's mug. 'You're not a kid. You make your own choices. Then you live by the results. That's simple enough. Trouble is, choices generally affect other people as well as yourself.'

He left the boy to mull it over. A minute later he returned from the kitchen with a pack of strong peppermints and a sprig of parsley.

'What are they for?' Richard asked.

Bergerac dropped them on the table. 'Just in case you'd rather not smell like a brewery.'

The boy unwrapped a peppermint and popped it in his

67

mouth. 'When do you want me to help with the car?' he asked.

'Saturday afternoon suit you?'

'OK.' Richard paused and then said in a rush, 'I tried to stop them, you know – at the off-licence. But . . .'

'It can be hard when there's a group of you.' Bergerac noticed that Richard's eyes had strayed away from his face. 'What are you looking at?'

'That picture – the little landscape. Do you mind if – ?'

Richard stood up and crossed the room to examine it. By now he was steady on his feet. He was also absorbed in what he was doing. For several minutes he said nothing. He looked at the painting from several angles. It was as if he had forgotten where he was.

'Brilliant,' he said at last. 'It's Mont Orgeuil, isn't it? Who did it?'

'Someone I used to know – her name's Francine Leland.'

'You *know* her?' Richard looked startled, as if he hadn't expected a copper to be sufficiently refined to have an artist among his friends. 'She's good,' he went on quickly, perhaps suspecting that his surprise was not altogether flattering to his host. 'I went to an exhibition of hers in St Malo last summer. I didn't know she did landscapes. I thought she was more into portraits.'

'She is.' Bergerac looked away. The picture had been Frankie's last present to him.

Richard, unaware that he was treading on an emotional minefield, plunged into what sounded like an informed critique of Frankie's work. Bergerac let him talk. The boy's face changed when it was alight with enthusiasm. He looked both older and more determined. When Richard ran out of steam, Bergerac stirred in his chair.

'You paint yourself?' he asked. 'Seriously, I mean?'

Richard's animation drained away. He studied Bergerac as if making up his mind about something.

'Of course I do,' he said. 'Actually, that's the real problem. With my parents, I mean.'

The desk sergeant concealed a smile behind his hand.

In his job, you saw a good range of eccentrics. The couple who had just come into the Bureau were a fine example of the breed. The man was in his seventies, at least; pink and scrubbed like a baby, he was clutching a pipe and looking over his shoulder for a way of escape. He was dwarfed by his companion – a skinny, angular woman who towed him along as though he were a recalcitrant toddler. She was probably in her fifties, but her clothes made her seem much older. The long skirt and high-necked blouse reminded the sergeant of photographs of suffragettes. A cameo brooch at the neck strengthened the similarity.

She strode up to the desk, tugging the man behind her.

'We wish to see Chief Inspector Crozier,' she announced in a booming voice. 'At once.'

It was the sort of voice that had been brought up to command obedience in a world that had now vanished. Before he knew it, the sergeant was on his feet.

'I'm afraid that's impossible, madam,' he said. 'The Chief Inspector's in conference all morning. And in the afternoon he's – '

'We can't wait that long.'

'Perhaps I can help?' the sergeant suggested without conviction.

The woman snorted. 'What about Mr Crozier's deputy? Who is the senior person at present in the Bureau?'

'That'd be Detective Sergeant Bergerac, madam. He – '

'Jim Bergerac?' The old man spoke for the first time. 'Yes, he'll do.' He patted his companion's arm. 'Jim's a nice fellow, Alex. We'll be all right with him.'

'A sergeant? Isn't there anyone of a higher rank available? I am not accustomed to dealing with sergeants.'

The desk sergeant ignored this. Scenting a way out for himself, he had already lifted the telephone.

'Your name, madam?' he asked; somehow there didn't seem much point in asking the man's.

'Miss Alexandra Irefield.'

'Jim?' he said into the phone. 'There's a Miss Irefield wants to see you . . . Yes, you could say that.' He glanced up at the old lady and swallowed. 'Yes, I'd say it's urgent.'

'Quite right, young man,' Miss Irefield said. 'It is.'

'George – haven't seen you for months. How are you keeping? I'm afraid Barney's tied up this morning. But I could send a message in to him if you want.'

Out of the corner of his eye, Bergerac could see the astonishment on the desk sergeant's face. The man had just missed a golden opportunity to be nice to the Chief Inspector's dad.

Bergerac was genuinely pleased to see the old man. George introduced him to his companion.

'This is Miss Irefield, Jim – she very kindly looks after my cottage for me.'

Bergerac shook hands with her. 'That's the one in St Ouen, isn't it? Somewhere near Plémont Bay?'

'That is correct, Sergeant. It is an excellent place for me to pursue my researches.'

'It's certainly lonely enough up there. What do you do?'

'I am a parapsychologist, Sergeant.' She met his eyes with a touch of defiance. 'The atmosphere is conducive to my work.'

'How can I help you?' Bergerac asked.

'Well, I'm not sure you can, Jim – '

'Nonsense, George! Either a crime has been committed or there's something very strange happening. It is essential that we discover which.'

'It just seems a bit of a wild-goose chase.' George looked pleadingly at Bergerac. 'I don't want to waste your time,

Jim. If Barney was here, that'd be different; he's family.' The old face cracked into a smile. 'He *has* to put up with me.'

Bergerac grinned at him. 'Well, now you're here, why not tell me. We needn't make it official unless you want to. What sort of crime?'

'Burglary?' George leant forward in his chair. 'To be honest, I'm not really sure.'

'Pull yourself together, George,' Miss Irefield ordered. 'Start at the beginning and go on to the end. It's always the best way.'

It was at that moment that Bergerac began to dislike Miss Irefield.

'I was coming back from Barney's last night,' the old man explained. 'Had a bite of supper with them, and Barney drove me back. It was raining hard and he didn't come in with me. I wish he had, now. You know where I live, Jim? Woodbridge House on Coleford Road. Two flats on each floor, and I'm on the top.' He chuckled unexpectedly. 'I always call it my penthouse.'

'I wish you'd get to the point,' Miss Irefield interrupted. 'I haven't got all day.'

He gave her an apologetic grimace. 'There was this bloke on my landing, just coming down. I asked if he wanted me, but he said, no, Number 7 – that's the other flat up there. Seemed in a bit of a hurry. The funny thing was, as he passed me on the stairs, I thought I recognized him. But I couldn't for the life of me put a name to him.'

'You'd better describe him,' Miss Irefield ordered.

'Not that big. In his forties, maybe. Dark hair. Wearing a light-coloured mac that was cut like a trench coat. Medium-posh voice, but somehow I don't think it came natural to him.'

'Go on about the door,' Miss Irefield said.

'Yes, the door.' George Crozier frowned. 'The thing is, it

71

was unlocked. And I'm pretty sure I locked it when I went out.'

'But not absolutely sure?' Bergerac said.

'Well, I'm a bit forgetful these days, I can't deny it. But then there was the curtains. They were drawn – and I think I left them open. I couldn't swear to it, mind.'

'Anything taken?'

George shook his head. 'I had a look round. Nothing was missing, as far as I could see.'

'How about the neighbours? Did you have a word with them?'

'They're away at present. He might have been a friend of theirs, I suppose. Young couple – I don't know them well.'

'Someone must have let him into the building,' Miss Irefield said. She glanced at Bergerac. 'They have one of those awful buzzing things on the front door.'

'Not necessarily, Alex. The front door doesn't always close properly, especially when it's wet. The wood's warped. And sometimes it gets left on the latch. Visitors quite often just walk right in.'

'It doesn't add up to much, does it?' Bergerac said gently. 'You meet a man on the stairs who could have been visiting someone else. Your door's unlocked and your curtains are drawn – but you might have left them that way yourself. Nothing was taken, as far as you know.'

'Tell him about the *man*,' Miss Irefield commanded.

'You remembered who he was, then?'

George Crozier nodded slowly. 'He's the spitting image of a bloke called Patrice Marigny.'

'And who's he when he's at home?'

'You could say he was a policeman.' George looked solemnly at Bergerac. 'The only snag is, if Marigny's alive, he's in his eighties by now.'

'So what are you saying? You saw a ghost or something?'

Miss Irefield was on to him immediately. 'The possibility

cannot be ruled out, Sergeant. If, as you obviously think, a burglary did not take place, we may well be dealing with a bona fide apparition.'

'Now, wait a minute – '

'I know what you're thinking.' Miss Irefield waved a finger at him. 'George lives in a post-war flat. How can a ghost haunt a place which didn't exist when it was alive?'

'Actually, I – '

'It's quite simple: ghosts, as you no doubt call them, can haunt people as well as places. Someone like George – an old man who has spent his whole life trying to pretend he isn't a sensitive – is particularly receptive. I would refer you to the Brennor case in Scunthorpe in 1933. Or, more recently, to the Zubriski Hauntings in Seattle in 1971. If an event or a person makes a deep emotional imprint, traces of it can last for years – if not for centuries. I can assure you that there is a substantial literature on the subject.'

'No doubt you're right, Miss Irefield. But isn't it rather more likely that there's a perfectly rational explanation for all this? Who was this Marigny in any case? When did you know him?'

'I never met him,' George said. 'Thank God.'

'*That*'s what makes the case potentially so interesting,' Miss Irefield remarked. 'I speak, of course, from a scientific point of view.'

'He was a Frenchman,' George went on. 'Seconded to the Gestapo during the war. Nasty type, by all accounts. He was responsible for the arrest of Henry Tillersland.'

Bergerac sighed. 'And who was he?'

'You don't know? Well, no reason why you should – you weren't even born. Nice old bloke – had a house on Wellington Road. Before the war I was his gardener and Marie was his cook. She stayed with him right through the war while I was in the army.'

'Why was he arrested?'

'He had a crystal set like everyone else. Also, he was part

73

Jewish.' George shook his head; he looked like a pink and puzzled owl. 'I never really understood what happened. The Gestapo picked him up a few weeks before liberation. And that was odd in itself, because by that stage they were lying low and trying to pretend they were just friendly neighbourhood bobbies; they weren't looking for trouble. Tillersland committed suicide during interrogation. Cyanide, I think it was.'

Bergerac tried to find firm ground among the morass of speculation. 'If you never met Marigny, how come you recognized him?'

'I've seen photographs. And Marie did a painting of him once. I've still got it somewhere – or rather, Barney has.'

'That's odd, isn't it? Painting Marigny, I mean.'

George shrugged. 'You don't understand, Jim. Painting Marigny was a way of trying to exorcize what he'd done. Marie hated him because she loved old Tillersland like a father. Hell, I was fond of him myself. *And* grateful to him.'

'OK, George.' Bergerac raised his hand as though to ward off the tide of useless information. 'Look, don't get me wrong – I'd like to help. But I don't think this is a police matter. There's no evidence that any crime's been committed.'

And precious little evidence of ghosts, either.

'I might have known.' Miss Irefield stood up. 'Typical of the official mind. You know what your trouble is, Sergeant? You're imprisoned by your own dogma. Come along, George.'

'Why not have a chat with Barney?' Bergerac said. 'Do you want me to mention it to him?'

'No, Jim – what's the use? He'd only say the same as you.'

'You'll have to tell your son,' Miss Irefield pointed out. 'We shall need that painting and any relevant photographs for our files.'

The old man hauled himself out of the chair. 'I don't know. Maybe I did imagine it all.'

'Easily done,' Bergerac said. 'I remember once I –'

'Nonsense!' Miss Irefield said. 'Your attitude, Sergeant, comes as no surprise to me. The police are always wilfully obtuse about these matters. Never mind, George. We shall conduct our own investigation.'

The desk sergeant looked up as the substantial shadow fell across the counter.

'Hello, Claude,' he said. 'How's the search for truth going?'

He cackled at his own wit.

Claude Yves smiled wearily; he was used to people cracking jokes at his expense.

'How's business?' he asked. His voice was a thin wheeze of air escaping with difficulty from a balloon of flesh. 'Anything I need to know?'

'Not really. Things are pretty slack at present – apart from the sex murders in Gorey.'

'Sex murders?' Yves said hopefully. His face fell. 'Don't tell me. You're having me on.'

The sergeant laughed again. 'Better luck tomorrow.'

'I need a story now,' Yves said. 'A man must live. And eat.'

'And drink, eh?'

Yves looked at his watch. 'Sometimes you come up with a good idea.'

'All right for some,' the sergeant grumbled. 'I reckon you spend ninety per cent of your working life in a bar.'

Yves was a freelance journalist who acted as the Jersey stringer for a number of mainland papers. He was a familiar figure at the Bureau and at the pubs patronized by off-duty policemen. Unlike the traditional fat man, he was always gloomy. He wore the same grubby, tweed suit, winter and summer; the material had been stretched out of shape by

75

its unremitting efforts to restrain the excess pounds within. Among the police and his fellow journalists, he was popularly known as Michelin Man.

Both the sergeant and Yves looked up as an ill-assorted couple came into reception from the offices.

'We could make an official complaint, of course,' the woman was saying. 'He really was most impertinent.'

'Now, Alex – don't take on,' her companion protested. 'Jim was only trying to do his job.'

'Who are they?' Yves muttered to the desk sergeant.

'The old battleaxe is called Miss Irefield,' the sergeant whispered. 'And guess who the old boy is – Barney Crozier's dad.'

'Oh, *really*?'

Miss Irefield paused, her hand on the door. 'The important question is whether or not there have been other sightings. Perhaps we should consider an appeal in the press.'

'I'm not sure Barney would like that.'

'Excuse me, Miss Irefield.' Yves wobbled across the foyer towards them. 'I couldn't help overhearing what you said. As it happens, I represent the press.'

The sergeant shook his head in reluctant admiration. You had to hand it to the old tub of lard: he never stopped trying to earn a living.

CHAPTER
7

That stupid old man!

Alice Crozier pushed down the accelerator as far as it would go. The red VW Polo roared up the short, steep drive and into the double garage. Barney's car was already there. At least he was home early for once – she would have someone to talk to. She braked sharply – just in time to prevent the car from crashing into her husband's Black and Decker Workmate.

How could he be so irresponsible?

She climbed out of the car and slammed the door. With the paper under her arm, she strode into the house. Barney was in the living-room, fiddling with the video.

'Hello, Alice.' He glanced up and then back to the book in which he noted the recordings he made. 'I just don't believe it. Do you know what Richard's done now? He's obliterated that documentary on the light-aircraft industry. And what have we got instead? Another bloody episode of *EastEnders*.'

Alice flung her briefcase on to the nearest chair. 'I presume you haven't seen this evening's paper?'

'No, I haven't. I just don't know what he sees in these soaps – do you? You'd think after all the – '

'Oh, never mind that,' she snapped. She tossed the *Jersey Evening Post* on to the carpet beside him. 'I suggest you take a look at page eleven.'

'Eh?'

'Page eleven, Barney.'

He looked up again. This time what he saw in her face made him scramble to his feet. 'The kids – are they OK?'

'It's not them,' she said bitterly. 'It's your father. There's no fool like an old fool. Go on, read it. WAR HERO SIGHTS GESTAPO GHOST.'

'Oh, my God.'

It was a half-page article, with photographs. Most of it was taken up with Claude Yves's interview with George Crozier and Alexandra Irefield – 'both prominent members of the Society for Psychical Research'. They made a lot of the fact that George had won the DCM at Alamein and the Military Medal in Italy. They even found the space to mention that George's son, Detective Chief Inspector Barney Crozier, was the head of the Bureau des Etrangers.

But Yves had really let himself go on Patrice Marigny:

> ... the Vichy Frenchman whose sinister personality dominated the Jersey Gestapo. Marigny, formerly a close associate of Klaus Barbie, is believed to have escaped from the island at the end of the war. Fearing the vengeance of the Allies, he may have assumed the identity of a sick private in hospital. It may be significant that, as a young man, he worked as an actor in Paris.
>
> There have been plenty of rumours about the war criminal's whereabouts. But nothing definite has been heard of him since the liberation, despite the authorities' unremitting efforts to track him down. Is it possible that he has finally died after a life under a false name? Mr Crozier and Miss Irefield are convinced that he has returned to haunt the island which was the scene of so many of his atrocities.
>
> Mr Crozier speculates that his involvement with the Tillersland family may be responsible for Marigny's posthumous interest in him. The death of Henry Tillersland was ...

They had dug up a photograph of Marigny from some-where. He was smiling at the camera, a cigarette in the corner of his mouth.

'That's the last time Michelin Man gets a story out of the Bureau,' Crozier said. 'I wonder who put him on to it.' He threw the paper on the floor and strode over to the sideboard. 'Do you want a drink?'

'Too early for me – Barney, did you know about this?'

'Jim said the old man had been into the Bureau yesterday with some rigmarole about burglars and Marigny. He was with that Irefield woman, apparently. Jim didn't take it seriously and nor did I. But I was going to phone Dad tonight.'

Alice's eyes narrowed. 'So you think Jim told Yves?'

Barney poured himself a large gin. 'I doubt it – not his style, you know.'

'I wish I could be as sure of that as you seem to be.'

'Jim's all right, Alice. Besides, he likes Dad and he doesn't like Yves. Damn it – have we run out of tonic?'

'There's some in the fridge. This is going to make us both look so *ridiculous*.'

'Do you think I don't know that?' Barney shouted from the kitchen. There was a crash as he dropped the ice tray.

'It's all right for you. But they're doing the short list for the assistant controller next week.'

Alice worked in the administration and planning section of the States Department of Social Security. If she got the promotion, she would effectively be in charge of the whole section.

'Well, what about me?' Barney was back in the sitting-room; his glass was already half empty. 'Can you imagine how those comedians on the Law and Order Committee will take this? I was hoping to get on the *ad hoc* subcommittee for liaison with the mainland. Do you think they'll want someone whose father sees ghosts?'

He took another swallow from his drink and sat down.

Alice sighed. 'It's a pity that Miss Irefield's involved. I knew that arrangement was a mistake.'

'It's Dad's cottage.' Barney's voice was weary: if he and Alice talked about his father, sooner or later the conversation would work its way round to this branch of the subject. 'He can do what he likes with it.'

'But you'd think he'd find a more constructive use for the place. And what does she pay him? About two quid a month?'

Barney shrugged. 'He's sorry for her, Alice – it's as simple as that. She's the original decayed gentlewoman. You know what he's like with lame dogs.'

'Lame parasites, if you ask me. It's obvious that she put him up to this. He'd never talk to the press on his own.'

'You're probably right.' Barney loosened his tie. The drink was beginning to improve his mood. In a moment he would pour himself another one. 'There's not a lot we can do about it now.'

'Damage limitation could help.'

'OK – I'll have a word with the old man, try and stop this going any further. Otherwise, all we can do is ride it out. It's not *that* bad, love. Even has its comic side.'

'I wish I could see the joke.' Alice's face softened. 'Your dad's just like one of the kids, really. We worry about him and try and look after him, we get irritated by him – you name it.'

'My mother used to say that Dad never grew up.'

'Talking of the kids – have you seen them since you got back?'

Barney shook his head. 'I hardly ever do.'

Alice frowned. 'I'm worried about Richard. I think you should have a word with him.'

'What is it this time?'

'You remember the night before last? When he came home late, after you'd gone to bed?'

Barney nodded.

'He looked as if he'd been fighting. I think he'd been drinking. And when I was putting his jeans in the washing-machine this morning, I found some cigarette papers in one of the pockets.'

Barney finished the drink. 'Tobacco? Or . . . ?'

'That's what worries me. I'm frightened it may be drugs.'

'Oh, God. That's all we need. But I'm sure I would have noticed.'

'Would you?'

They stared at one another.

'A ghost!' Mrs Arkwright cackled. 'George took you for a ghost!'

'Don't go on about it, Mother.'

They were sitting in the hire-car at the bottom of the road where the Croziers lived. Mrs Arkwright had the *Post* on her lap. She had forced Winston to read her every word in the article.

'I told you you were like him. You didn't believe me, did you?'

'It's just as well I am,' Arkwright said. 'Otherwise the police might start asking awkward questions.'

'I wonder how George knew. He wasn't on the island during the war.'

'Shut up, Mother. I think that's the son.'

Richard Crozier cycled slowly up the avenue. He was wearing jeans and a loose, black T-shirt covered with swastikas. The evening wasn't warm, but he hadn't bothered with a jacket – presumably because he thought it would obscure the glory of the T-shirt. He left the bike in the garage and went into the house.

'He's at the rebellious stage, I should think,' Arkwright said thoughtfully. 'Might come in useful.'

His mother patted his arm. 'Sometimes you don't just look like your dad. You even think like him.'

At that moment the shouting began.

Mrs Arkwright wound down her window a little further. 'A family row?' she murmured.

The windows at the front of the Croziers' house were open. You could hear the raised voices, though it was impossible to distinguish any words. The quarrel was brief but – to judge by the sound of breaking glass – dramatic.

Richard Crozier stormed out of the house. He ran into the garage, grabbed his bicycle and free-wheeled down the drive.

His father appeared in the doorway. 'Now, come here, Richard.' He tried to keep his voice reasonably low.

The boy swung out into the road and began to pedal furiously.

'I said, *come here*!' Crozier yelled. 'If you don't – '

Suddenly he retreated into the house and slammed the front door.

Arkwright laughed.

'What are you waiting for?' his mother said. 'Follow the boy.'

The pub was in a side-street off Belmont Road. Richard had been there before, though never by himself. You got to know the establishments where they weren't too particular about the age of their customers.

He padlocked the bicycle to a railing and unstrapped his jacket from the pillion. The jacket made him look older, he thought, especially when he turned the collar up.

His conscience chose that moment to remind him what had happened the last time he went drinking. He pushed the memory aside. What did Bergerac know about it anyway? He was just a has-been alcoholic.

The pub smelled of stale beer and old men. It was a small, dark room, whose once white ceiling had dulled to a nicotine yellow. There were no other customers apart from two pensioners at the table by the window. Holding himself as tall as possible, Richard walked up to the bar. A couple came in behind him. The landlord was engrossed in the *Jersey Evening Post*.

'A pint of lager, please.'

The old man looked up. He had a square face, seamed with lines and much the same colour as his ceiling.

'How old are you, son?'

Richard felt himself flushing. 'Eighteen,' he said firmly.

'Got proof of that, have you?'

'Of course my grandson's eighteen,' a woman said behind him. 'We also want a large Scotch and a large port and lemon.'

Richard swung round. The old lady gave him a benevolent smile. Beside her was a middle-aged man in dark glasses.

'Let's go and sit down,' she said. 'Your father will bring the drinks.'

'Sorry,' the landlord said. 'Didn't realize he was with you.' He reached for the glasses. 'Have to be careful, you understand. You know what kids are like today.'

'Of course you do,' the man agreed. 'Ice with the Scotch, please. Have one yourself.'

The woman led the way to a table at the back of the bar. As she moved, her white cane swung to and fro in front of her, clicking against the legs of tables and chairs and scraping on the uncarpeted floor. They sat down. Richard held the chair for her.

'I'm not entirely blind,' she said. 'Not yet.'

'I . . . I'm glad,' Richard said. He added, a second later, 'Thanks.'

'They can be so stupid, can't they? Landlords, I mean. I used to have just the same trouble, even after I'd married.'

His rescuer introduced herself as Mrs Smilie. Her son arrived with their drinks. Richard's opinion of his hosts soared even higher when he had his first sip. The man had got him the most expensive lager in the house.

As they drank, they talked. By the time they were on the second round, Richard had become almost eloquent. His new friends seemed to find his conversation fascinating. He told them things he would never have mentioned at home; for some reason it was easier to talk to strangers. Once or twice he suspected he must be boring them and tried to turn the conversation round to them, but each time Mrs Smilie deflected his question and asked another one about him.

With the third drink he found himself talking about the latest row with his parents. They were very sympathetic – the old woman especially. It was almost like talking to someone of his own age.

'What did you say your father's name was?'

Richard wasn't aware that he had mentioned it. But, fogged with alcohol, he couldn't be sure.

'Barney Crozier,' he said. 'Why?'

'And he's a copper?'

'Detective Chief Inspector.' Richard could remember a time, not so long ago, when he had been proud of that.

'*Well!*' Mrs Smilie turned to her son. 'Would you believe it? Who says coincidences don't happen?'

It was nearly midnight when they dropped him in Beaumont, at the bottom of the road where the Croziers lived.

Arkwright helped the boy retrieve his bicycle from the boot of the car.

He and his mother watched as Richard walked up the hill towards retribution, wheeling his bicycle. He only stumbled once. Several times he turned and waved to them. Arkwright started the engine, made a three-point turn and drove away.

'He's not *too* pissed, is he?' he said. 'We don't want his parents to start an international incident.'

'He's OK. The meal will have sobered him up. He only had Coke after the third pint.'

Arkwright glanced at his mother as he drove. 'Do you think he'll do it?'

She shrugged. 'It's worth trying. Think of the risk it'll save.'

He grunted. 'There's a burglar alarm on the house. I couldn't cope with that. But you have to admit it's a long shot – and in more ways than one.'

'Stop worrying, will you?'

'But he might tell his parents!'

'He won't. In any case, we're safe. He doesn't know who we are or where we're staying.'

'How can you be so sure he won't talk?'

She massaged the head of her cane and laughed. It was not a pleasant sound.

'You forget, Winston. I know what men are like. Teenagers, young men, middle-aged and bloody geriatrics. I've known them all.'

CHAPTER
8

In the modern world, financial institutions offer their customers a wide range of services. The better the customer, the wider the range.

Leonard Silbermann of the Vanguard Trust Corporation was a firm believer in the importance of keeping his clients happy. A happy client meant a happy firm; a happy firm meant a happy Leonard Silbermann.

He ringed the article in the *Jersey Evening Post* with a felt-tip pen. He tapped the word 'DULOV' into the keyboard of his personal computer. The disk drive whirred. The VDU screen filled with a mass of figures.

Yes, it was certainly worth making an effort for Dulov. And, even if one put professional considerations aside (which was, of course, impossible), there were strong reasons in favour of making that little extra effort for an important customer.

Dulov was not the sort of man who forgot a favour. Moreover, Silbermann approved of what Dulov was doing. The world was forgetting too soon. It was good that someone remembered.

He tapped another command into the computer. Words replaced the numbers. He could telex the contents of the article to the office Dulov maintained in Geneva; that would be the easiest way. But the man was in the States at present, and the information might be urgent.

Silbermann buzzed for his secretary and then remembered that she had long since gone home. Perhaps it was all to the good. Jersey was a bit too close to home for comfort. It might be better if no one in the office was aware of the call.

He got up and searched the files himself. As he had thought, Dulov had sent them a copy of his itinerary in case the negotiations for the oil leases needed a quick decision. Right now he was in Washington – no doubt badgering one of his CIA informants. Silbermann admired perseverance. It got you everywhere. Eventually.

This time Dulov was travelling under the name of Fisher. Silbermann made a note of the phone number. He used his private, direct line; that way the call would not be logged by the computer that was linked to the Vanguard switchboard.

Silbermann struck lucky first time: Dulov was in his room and he was answering his phone.

'Yosef? This is Leonard. Sorry to trouble you, but there's an item in our local paper which might interest you.'

'Your work or mine?' Dulov was always careful on the phone.

'Yours.' Silbermann took a deep breath and decided to risk a name. 'An old man in St Helier saw Marigny the other night.'

There was a chuckle on the other end of the line. 'That is impossible.'

'Yes, I know. But an explanation occurred to me. Just an idea, you understand. I remember you saying that Marigny might have left something here. He was in such a hurry to leave, wasn't he?'

'True.'

'Well – what if there were a son? He might want to pick up his – ah – inheritance.'

'Perhaps you would send me the text of this news item.'

'Of course,' Silbermann said eagerly. 'I'll get it off right away.'

'Good. Thank you, Leonard.'

And the line went dead.

CHAPTER
9

His head felt as if it belonged to someone else. Someone he didn't like.

He moved it cautiously on the pillow. A stabbing pain zigzagged across his forehead, temporarily dwarfing the background ache. His tongue had doubled in size overnight. He was very thirsty.

A lavatory flushed; the noise made him wince. Couldn't they be quieter? Footsteps clattered down the stairs. Somewhere a door banged. A car engine came noisily to life.

Without warning his door opened.

His father stuck his head into the room. 'Aren't you up yet? You'll be late for school.'

Richard closed his eyes.

His father dragged the duvet off him. 'Get up, will you?'

Sullenly Richard swung his feet over the side of the bed. The headache retaliated by becoming almost blinding in its intensity.

'We're going to talk this evening,' his father said. 'Right?'

'Right,' Richard echoed wearily. *You'll lecture and I'll listen. As usual.*

'Well, get a move on.' His father glanced at his watch. 'I'll have to go. There's some tea in the pot.'

The door slammed behind him. Richard padded into the bathroom for a glass of water and the aspirin. Then he got back into bed and pulled the duvet up to his chin. Yesterday flooded back into his mind. The memory of the two rows with his parents – one at the beginning of the evening, the other at the end – mingled in his mind with the hangover.

School – well, sod that.

It had been quite an evening, what with one thing and another. Old Mrs Smilie was a good sort and she'd talked a lot of sense. It was typical that his parents wouldn't even let her see the family papers, which rightfully belonged to her.

He wondered if Grandad had ever met her. Mrs Smilie was a Tillersland by birth, a cousin of the Henry Tillersland that Grandad was always going on about. Richard had been brought up with the idea that Henry Tillersland was a kind of fairy godmother to the Crozier family; although he was dead, his good deeds lived on.

Grandad and Grandma used to work for Tillersland. When he died, he left his money to his son, but the son had already been killed in Normandy and Grandad and Grandma were the old man's next heirs. That's how Grandad had been able to buy the market garden after he was demobbed from the army. And that was why they had the cottage.

It was unfair really – the money should have gone to Mrs Smilie; she was a blood relative. But she wanted nothing from his parents except a piece of her own family history. And they wouldn't let her have it.

It was typical of them – *typical*.

Richard's eyelids closed.

When he woke for the second time it was after half-past ten. He felt much better. He stretched luxuriously, determined to wring every last drop of pleasure out of this day of truancy. He began the day with a long, hot bath. Downstairs he made a pot of real coffee. He drank it black and without sugar. He was training himself to like it that way. He tried to roll a cigarette, but gave this up after the third failure.

Then he set to work.

He went up to the spare bedroom over the garage. His father used it as a study. Like everything else his father had anything to do with, the room was immaculately tidy.

The tin box was in the lowest drawer of the desk. Richard remembered his parents talking about it when Grandad gave it to them.

Just family papers. The old man thought I might as well have them now.

He lifted out the box. It was locked, but the key was tied to the handle with wire. The lid came up with a screech of rusty metal.

The first thing he saw was a black-and-white studio photograph of a pretty young woman. It took him a moment to realize he was looking at his grandmother. For the first time it occurred to him that he was trespassing in other people's pasts.

One by one he lifted out the contents. He lingered over a folder of small, unframed watercolours. Most of them were portraits and all of them were good. He didn't go in for naturalism himself, but he could appreciate it in others. The technique was crude in places, but all the pictures were alive. The young bloke in a sergeant's uniform had to be Grandad. The only clue to the artist was a minute 'MC' pencilled at the bottom of each painting.

Marie Crozier? Grandma painted and they never told me?

He quarried deeper into the box. Letters, more photographs, certificates – his sense of guilt grew with each discovery; these were someone else's secrets. He examined none of them, beyond a cursory glance to make sure that they had nothing to do with the Tillerslands.

At the very bottom was a bundle of yellowing papers, tied with a fraying ribbon and with 'Tillersland' written on the outside in faded black ink. He seized them with relief. There weren't many papers in the enclosure. Mrs Smilie could photocopy them in no time.

He stuffed the other items back into the box. Doubts and

questions poured into his mind, but he blocked them off with the thought that his parents had no right to deprive an old woman of a few harmless memories. He returned the box to the drawer.

He crammed the Tillersland bundle into the inside pocket of his jacket. Mrs Smilie had said she would meet him in the same pub off Belmont Road at lunchtime. There was plenty of time.

The doubts and the questions returned as he walked downstairs. What had Bergerac said the other night? Something about adults having to take the consequences of the decisions they made?

But if he was doing the right thing, why the hell did he feel so guilty?

'I've just remembered. I left the list of queries at home. Not that I did any work on them last night.'

'No problem,' Bergerac said. 'It's on the way – we'll pick them up.'

The two men strolled into the car-park outside police headquarters. Crozier moaned as the bright sunshine hit his eyes.

'Do you mind if we go in your car?'

'Sure – if you want.' Bergerac glanced at him. 'You OK, Barney? You're looking a bit peaky.'

'I just don't feel like driving.' Crozier lowered himself into the Triumph. 'The last thing I want to do is look at rows of figures. If you must know, I had a few too many last night. And now I've got a permanent headache.'

Bergerac raised his eyebrows. 'Celebrating?'

'More like drowning our sorrows.'

'In the shape of the family ghost?'

'Not just that. We had a couple of flaming arguments with Richard. Then Alice and I stayed up for hours, trying to work out what we'd done wrong. You know the sort of thing. You must have gone through it with Kim.'

'Wrong tense.' Bergerac started the engine. 'That sort of thing seems to go on for ever.'

Out of deference to the fragile condition of his passenger, Bergerac drove sedately out of St Helier in the St Aubin direction. He wasn't looking forward to this afternoon either. The Bureau's quarterly accounts were being prepared. This involved an independent auditor scrutinizing the figures, both at the draft stage and in their final form. Regulations insisted that two officers from the Bureau should be present at all discussions with the auditor.

The Croziers lived on a comfortable new estate with good views over the bay. Their road was packed with parked cars. A Volvo blocked the access to Crozier's drive.

'So they're all three-car families round here, are they?'

Crozier scowled. 'That damned woman at Number 5 is having another of her Tupperware parties. One day I'm going to make a formal complaint. Try the sidé-road after our house.'

Bergerac found a parking slot and pulled in.

'Want some coffee?' Crozier said. 'We're early and I'm parched.'

'OK. You're the boss.'

To Crozier's surprise, half a pot of coffee was standing in the coffee-making machine. It was still hot. He poured himself a mug and sipped it.

'A bit stewed, but it's drinkable. Richard must have made it this morning.'

He gave Bergerac a mug and led the way upstairs. Bergerac leant against the door jamb.

Crozier frowned. 'There's a coffee ring on my blotter.'

'A detective,' Bergerac said drily, 'is on duty at *all* times.'

'Yes, but it's odd . . . It wasn't there last night. Richard must have been in here.'

He pulled open the centre drawer and took out a manila folder. 'Here we are. Oh, and while I'm here – there's something my father wanted.'

As Bergerac watched, Crozier opened the bottom drawer and lifted out a tin box. He unlocked it and pulled up the lid.

'It's the family archive,' he said over his shoulder. 'Dad passed it on to me – I've never even seen inside it.'

He lifted out the contents, one by one. 'Here we are. Want to see some pictures?'

Bergerac came forward. Crozier pulled half a dozen watercolours from a folder and laid them face upwards on the desk. The colours were still vivid. One of them was of a big Victorian house set in a sloping garden. The others were portraits. They were of varying sizes, though none was larger than six inches by eight. Each of them was meticulously detailed.

Bergerac whistled. 'Why don't you have these up on your wall. They're good, Barney – really good. Who did them?'

'My mother, believe it or not. I never even knew she painted until Dad mentioned it the other night. Look – that's the one he wants.'

Crozier pointed at a head and shoulders portrait of a dark-haired man in a grey suit. He had a long face with heavily marked features. A cigarette in a holder projected at a jaunty angle from his mouth.

'Looks like an off-duty clown,' Bergerac said. 'Who is he?'

'Marigny.'

'Not quite the Gestapo stereotype, is he? How did your mother come to do it?'

'It was after the war – from a photograph and from memory.'

'You'd have thought she'd have wanted to forget him.'

Crozier grunted and dug deeper into the box. 'He wanted some stuff about Tillersland as well. There should be a bundle somewhere.'

'Is that the place where he lived?' Bergerac was examining the Victorian house. 'Wellington Road?'

Crozier nodded. 'It's a small hotel now. Most of the garden's been built over. Where the hell is that bundle?'

Downstairs a door opened and closed.

Crozier looked up with a frown.

There were footsteps on the stairs. Crozier and Bergerac instinctively moved away from the open door of the study. Alice was at work and the kids were at school.

Then Richard Crozier came through the doorway. He was breathing heavily. In one hand was a carrier-bag; in the other was a bundle of yellowing papers held together by a ribbon.

When he saw the reception committee he stopped short. His eyes flicked from his father to Bergerac and then down to the floor.

'What are you doing here?' Crozier demanded. 'You're meant to be at school.'

Bergerac cleared his throat. 'I think I'll have another coffee,' he said to no one in particular. 'I'll be downstairs.'

He slipped out of the room. Even in the kitchen he could hear the raised voices.

'You – you bastard!' Richard yelled. 'I'll never forgive you. *Never!*'

On his way home from work that evening, Crozier stopped off in Coleford Road.

His father was expecting him.

'You all right, Barney?' he said as he led the way into the living-room. 'You look like you've been having too many late nights.'

Barney ignored the question. He sat down and opened his briefcase. 'There's the painting.' He passed it to George. 'And here's the Tillersland stuff.'

'Thanks.' George studied the portrait. 'Plausible-looking bloke, wasn't he? And he's identical to the chap I saw.'

'Dad – will you promise me something?'

'Eh?'

'Don't get too involved with this. It's bad news for all of us.'

George sighed. 'I'm not that keen myself. But Alex says – '

'She's a meddling old woman with a taste for publicity,' Barney interrupted. 'I wish she'd get off the island.'

His father's face was suddenly stern. 'She's also my friend,' he said gently. 'And she needs help.'

Barney looked away. His father's reproofs had always been rare. As he grew older, they became rarer still. Against all reason, they still had the power to make Barney feel guilty. *Why can't I talk to Richard like that?*

'Sorry,' he muttered. 'I didn't mean to . . .'

'You're right, of course. I'll try and keep her away from the press.'

'Thanks.'

'Let's have a drink,' George said. 'You know where to find the Scotch.'

As Barney poured the drinks, George relit his pipe and opened the Tillersland bundle. He leafed through the contents. Barney put the glasses on the table between their chairs.

'You haven't looked at these?' his father said.

'No.'

George frowned. 'Something's missing, you see. It was a letter which Henry wrote to his son. He left it with your mother.'

'For David Tillersland? Wasn't he dead?'

'Henry didn't know that.'

'What was in it?'

'No idea. We never opened it.'

Barney blinked. 'Why not, for God's sake?'

The old man shrugged. 'None of our business what Henry had to say to David. Your mother thought there was maybe a chance that David might not be dead. Did you know his body was never recovered? There was an explosion, you see . . . No real doubt about his death, but strange things happen in war. So we just kept the letter, in case he turned up.'

'Well, I'll be damned. And it's not there?'

George shook his head.

'I'd better tell you.' Barney took a long swallow of his drink. 'I was hoping it was nothing . . .'

'What *are* you talking about?'

'Richard.'

Barney described what had happened that afternoon. 'He had the Tillersland papers in his hand. I think he was going to put them back in the box, and no one would have been the wiser. He wouldn't say what he wanted with them. And why the Tillersland stuff – I could understand if it had been Mum's paintings or something.'

'Do you think he took the letter?'

'Search me. There was another thing. He'd been on a spending spree. That bag was full of brushes and paints and God knows what. I found the receipt. Over forty quid. In cash. Now where the hell did he get that kind of money?'

'What did he say when you asked him?'

'Nothing. Just clammed up. I've met some obstinate customers in my time, but he takes the cake.'

George's eyes were troubled. 'He's very like you.'

'Come off it, Dad.'

'It's true, Barney. You're just the same even now. You'll be led, but you won't be driven. And if someone tries to drive you, then God help the driver.'

His mother was home.

She had brought him a cup of tea and a sandwich, but she wouldn't talk. He had never seen her so angry. When his father came back, they'd haul him downstairs and give him the state trial treatment.

He hadn't talked. He was proud of that.

96

And this is for you, Mrs Smilie had said when she gave him the envelope with the money in it.

But I don't want it.

I know you don't, lad. But you deserve it. It's a present. My way of saying 'thank you'.

She had asked him not to mention the photocopying to his parents, explaining that it would be embarrassing both for them and for her. Why should Mrs Smilie be embarrassed? She didn't deserve that on top of everything else.

No. He wouldn't tell them. If they wanted to have a state trial, they could do it without the prisoner in the dock.

Richard scrambled off the bed and opened the built-in wardrobe. His face was hard: had he but known it, he looked astonishingly like his father.

He took out a rucksack. He packed it methodically. There was no sense in rushing into anything.

Like his father, Richard was a careful planner.

Mrs Arkwright had a taste for Black Velvet.

Perched on a stool, she was on her third when her son came into the Marine Bar of the Hôtel de Bretagne.

'I'm celebrating,' she said when Arkwright tried to prevent her from ordering another.

'We've a long way to go,' he hissed. 'You're being a little premature.'

'You're just jealous,' she said with a cackle. 'I got the letter from the boy. Not you.'

'All right, Mother.' He changed tack and tried to coax her. 'You did brilliantly. But Richard's not going to keep his mouth shut – you can bet on that.'

'So what? They can't trace us.'

'I wouldn't be so sure. He's seen us both, and we don't exactly blend in with the crowd.'

'Have a drink and stop worrying.'

To shut her up, Arkwright bought them both a drink and steered her away to a secluded table.

'I've rented a flat for us. It'll be much more private. Much safer altogether.'

She made less fuss than he had expected.

'But I'm still worried about Barney Crozier. He's a copper, after all. He must have his suspicions about the ghost business. Once he finds out about the letter . . .'

His mother patted his had. 'You're such a worrier, Winston. Always were and always will be. But I've had another idea. We're not going to have any problems with Barney. Not now and not ever.'

CHAPTER
10

The day started innocently enough.

Bergerac drove straight from home to St Brelade to follow up an anonymous complaint that a restaurant was mistreating its immigrant staff. It didn't take long to sort out the problem. The staff were happy enough – well paid and well looked after. But one of the chefs had been fired last week for selling supplies on the side. The manager didn't want to prosecute because he wasn't the revengeful type. The chef didn't have such a forgiving nature.

The chef, now suitably contrite, got off with a warning. Bergerac drove back along the coast to the Bureau. A few hardy swimmers had been tempted into the sea. It was a fine April day – the sort that fooled you into thinking that summer was just round the corner. He parked at headquarters and went into the Bureau.

He knew something was wrong as soon as he reached the main office. People were standing in groups of two and three, talking in hushed voices. Crozier's door was closed. Peggy Masters fluttered towards him like an agitated hen.

'Whose funeral?' Bergerac asked.

'It's not a joke, Jim. Richard Crozier's missing.'

'Run away from home?'

She nodded. 'Yesterday evening.'

'Well, he can't have gone far. Has Barney made this official?'

'First thing this morning.' Peggy hesitated. 'Jim, the Chief Inspector's really upset. I've never seen him like this.'

There was a stir in the doorway. "'Scuse me,' a voice wheezed behind them.

Bergerac and Peggy moved aside. An elderly man wheeled a trolley into the office. He was a former constable, invalided out of the force on the grounds of ill health. Now he spent his working life distributing the mail, both internal and external, throughout the whole building.

He paused by Peggy and pointed at two piles on the top layer of the trolley. 'These are for Mr Crozier and those are for you.' He shook his head with gloomy relish. 'Sad news, Mrs Masters. You can never tell with kids these days. I shouldn't be surprised if it's drugs.'

'Nonsense, Stan. It's just a teenage prank, that's all.'

'It's not what they're saying in the canteen.' By virtue of his job, Stan had access to every gossip network in the building. 'Miss Hinksey reckons he's had an accident while under the influence. If you ask me, they'll have to get the dogs out.'

'But I'm *not* asking you, Stan,' Peggy said with some asperity.

'How's Mr Crozier taking it?'

Peggy glanced at her watch. 'Aren't you running late?'

Stan gave her up as a bad job.

Peggy went through the two bundles. 'I can deal with most of these. I don't really want to bother Mr Crozier at a time like this. But he'll need that file, I'm afraid. And there's a letter marked "Personal and Confidential".'

'I'll take them in,' Bergerac said. 'I need a word with him in any case.'

He tapped on Crozier's door and stuck his head inside.

'Come in, Jim. You've heard?'

Bergerac nodded. 'I'm sorry, Barney – I really am. Have you had any news?'

'I've got a team working on it – contacting Richard's friends. Uniformed and CID are being very helpful, for once. Wilson just phoned in – he's been checking the harbour and the airport.'

'Did Richard have that kind of money?'

Crozier put his head in his hands. 'I don't know. He's my own son and, God help me, I don't know.'

Bergerac had some idea of what Crozier was going through. Kim had once been kidnapped. He could remember that anguished sense of helplessness only too well.

He pulled up a chair and sat down. 'Took his passport, did he?'

'Yes. No trace of him at the airport, but he might have gone to the mainland on the overnight ferry. Wilson's trying to check it out. Trouble is, that particular boat was overflowing with kids of about his age. Some big drama festival in – '

The phone cut him off in mid-sentence. He grabbed the handset.

Peggy's crisp voice was clearly audible to Bergerac. 'I have Charlie Hungerford on the line for you, sir. Shall I put him through?'

'Not unless he's got anything useful to say,' Crozier snarled.

'I rather doubt it.'

'Then tell him I'm engaged. No calls unless . . .'

'I understand, sir.'

Crozier slammed down the phone. 'The vultures are gathering,' he said bitterly. 'Peggy's already had to fend off Michelin Man. Where were we?'

'The overnight ferry,' Bergerac said. 'But my guess is that he's still on the island. Don't worry – we'll find him.'

'I could kick myself. If I'd reported him missing last night – '

'Don't blame yourself. You thought he'd be back in an hour or two, looking sheepish?'

'That's what we wanted to believe, I suppose. But

Richard was always pigheaded. I just don't know where he gets it from.'

Bergerac decided that now was not the moment to enlighten him.

Crozier made a painfully obvious effort to pull himself together. He held out his hand. 'Those for me?'

'Oh – I nearly forgot. Peggy asked me to drop them in.'

Crozier worked through the pile, tossing most of the items into the pending-tray. But he opened the envelope marked 'Personal and Confidential'. Even at a time like this, he slit the flap neatly with a ruler.

He pulled out the contents. Bergerac glimpsed a black-and-white photograph and a brief typewritten note. Crozier stared at them for a few seconds and then thrust them back in the envelope. Maybe it was a trick of the light, but he looked paler than before.

'Did you check out the tip-off from St Brelade?'

Business as usual?

Crozier's voice was normal, but Bergerac could just see his right hand round the side of the desk; the fingers clenched and unclenched as if they were trying to throttle an invisible orange.

Bergerac explained quickly what had happened. He then asked if there was anything he could do in connection with the hunt for Richard.

'Thanks, but no.' Crozier ran his fingers through his hair. 'You've got your own workload. There are far too many people on this already. We should be treating this as an ordinary missing-person case.'

Bergerac stood up. 'There's no way we can do that, Barney,' he said with his hand on the door. 'So just let me know if I can help. OK?'

'OK – if and when. And Jim?'

'What?'

Crozier studied his nails. 'Er – thanks.'

As Bergerac left the office, the phone began to ring once more.

He passed Peggy's desk on the way to his own. She was just putting down her own phone.

Her face was worried. 'She wouldn't give her name, but I put her through. I hope I did the right thing.'

'Someone for Barney?'

'It sounded like an old woman. It was most peculiar. She said she had some private family information for him and that it was most urgent. I said, was it about Richard. And she said, no, not directly – more about the Chief Inspector's *mother*.'

'Barney Crozier?'

'Yes – who is this?'

'Never mind, Barney, never mind. Just listen to me.'

'I'm afraid you'll have to – '

'You've seen the photograph, haven't you? You've read my note?'

'*You* sent them? What are you trying to do?'

'The shock could kill your father. And it won't do you much good, or your wife and children. Just listen to me, Barney.'

The voice on the other end of the line had no name and no discernible regional accent. Old and female, yes; that was all you could say about it, apart from one other adjective, which had nothing to do with age or sex.

Crozier tried to put the word out of his head. It was a subjective and emotional label – totally valueless to the rational mind. But the word refused to leave him alone.

The voice was evil.

There was no other word for it.

'Are you listening carefully? That's your mother in that photograph. You probably knew that. She's wearing that big garnet brooch your dad gave her before the war – the one in the shape of a knot. Look carefully, Barney – can you see it?'

The photograph lay before him on the desk. Crozier looked at it through a magnifying glass. The woman was right. Alice had the brooch now, though she never wore it. The old man had given it to her after Marie Crozier's death.

'Yes,' he said hoarsely. 'I can see it.'

'And you recognize her gentleman friend, don't you? *Very* friendly they are. You see how she's clinging on to his arm and staring *deep* into his eyes? That's Patrice Marigny, Barney. After the war they said he'd committed crimes against humanity. That's a laugh, isn't it?'

There was a cackle like the rustle of paper at the other end of the line.

'There must be some mistake – '

'No mistake, Barney. Now, here's a riddle. There's one person in that photograph that you can't see. And he's alive today. Where is he?'

Crozier said nothing. He pulled open the centre drawer, looking for the tape recorder that could be plugged into the phone. The drawer was empty. The engineers had taken it away for the annual service.

'Give up? He's in your mother's stomach, boy. And when he came out in January '46, your mother gave him a name. She called him *Barney*. Now do you understand?'

'You're out of your mind.'

'Be a man and face it – you're a bastard, Barney. George isn't your dad. Your mother was a whore. And your real father? Well, you know what they said about people like him at Nuremberg.'

'You can't prove anything.'

'Oh, but I can. The photograph will help. And there's a letter.'

'A letter?' Before he could stop himself he added, 'Tillersland?'

104

'You're getting there, Barney. I must say, you're a slow thinker for a copper.'

'Do you know where Richard is?'

'Richard?' For the first time there was a note of surprise in the voice. 'How should I know? What's happened to him?'

'He . . . he left home last night.'

There was a moment's silence. Crozier wiped his sweating hand on his trousers. Even the rumour of this could kill his father; the old man had a heart condition. *My father? Who is my father?* And how would it affect Alice and her job, not to mention her political ambitions?

How would it affect himself?

'Look,' he said, lowering his voice to a whisper. 'What do you want?'

'I thought you'd be sensible, Barney. Your father was a very sensible man by all accounts. Just listen and I'll tell you.'

CHAPTER

II

The man who was travelling under the name of Fisher slipped into the departure lounge at Bristol Airport.

He was a tall man – well over six feet – with gangling limbs, which belonged to a larger torso than he possessed. He had curly hair, originally red but now heavily powdered with grey. He was dressed in a sombrely expensive suit and shoes that were probably handmade.

The Dan Air flight to Jersey was already boarding, so he was in the departure lounge for the shortest possible time. It was the sheerest bad luck that someone noticed him.

That afternoon there were two Special Branch officers in the departure lounge of every commercial airport in the United Kingdom. None of them was looking for a man travelling under the name of Fisher.

One of the officers nudged his colleague. 'I know that bloke, Jack.'

'The tall one?' All the colleague could see was the rear view of a man sidling towards the short-haul turbo-prop 748 on the runway. 'He doesn't look *quite* like one of ours.'

There was a distinct note of sarcasm in his voice. The nationwide Special Branch activity was directed at a pair of Irish terrorists who were believed to be leaving the country. Both of them were stocky men and neither came within several inches of six feet.

'Yeah – I know.'

The first officer fell silent. But he was a good policeman. The incident continued to irritate his mind. He stopped at the Dan Air desk on the way out. The woman remembered the passenger since he was the last to check in.

He had an American passport and his name was Jerome Fisher.

The officer made a note of the passport number.

CHAPTER
12

Miss Irefield plodded up the lane. By this stage it had narrowed to a mere path. The shopping bag in her right hand made her feel as though one leg was shorter than the other. She was thinking about mud.

There was mud everywhere. The shortcut to the cottage was more like a drainage ditch than a thoroughfare. It had rained earlier today and the water had collected in murky puddles. The mud tried to suck off her Wellington boots at every step. One side of her tweed skirt was stained with mud from when she had slipped. The skirt would need dry-cleaning. It was another expense she could not afford.

She regretted now that she hadn't taken the car. It was a mile to the village shop by road. She had wanted to economize on petrol. Thanks to the mud, it had proved to be a false economy.

Soon she would have to say goodbye to the Morris Minor. It gobbled money. For twenty-seven years she had cherished that car, and in return it had given her mobility and independence. But it was already overdue for a service, and tax and insurance would have to be paid in June. Quite impossible. It would be back to Shanks's Pony for her. Back to plodding through the mud.

The path levelled out and ran in a curve through a small copse of stunted trees and tangled bushes. As she emerged from the copse, the full force of the wind hit her for the first time. Beyond the cliffs stretched the endless grey sea. The sucking and smacking of the waves mixed with the cries of gulls. It was going to be a rough night.

Elizabeth Cottage was sixty yards away, perched on the high ground before the land began its precipitous fall to the cliffs. It was a box-like structure built of granite and facing south, away from the sea. At one end was a lean-to cowshed, now inhabited by the Morris Minor. A windswept garden surrounded the cottage.

Miss Irefield studied the house with a mixture of relief and loathing as she drew closer. At least George kept the place structurally sound. It was a pity he wouldn't do something about the inside. The garden was a burden, which she had no intention of shouldering. Still, Elizabeth Cottage was home. She supposed she should be grateful.

It was a relief to be out of the wind and into the warmth. The stove, rather to Miss Irefield's surprise, was still alight. She put the kettle on – it was the first of the tasks she had ordained for herself. Miss Irefield divided her life into a series of tasks.

While the kettle was boiling, she changed her clothes and put away the shopping. She hummed as she moved from room to room. She used the former living-room, next to the kitchen, as her study. It was lined with bookshelves – unpainted pine planks supported by piles of bricks. Hanging behind the door was the 35 mm camera with which she had once captured incontrovertible visual evidence of the Witcham Vicarage ghost. The photograph had made the front page of the *Psychic Review*. Only the blinkered scepticism of the media had prevented it from appearing in the nationals.

The sight of her desk gave her pleasure. Pride of place was given to the two box files that contained her current work: one, labelled 'Jersey Ghosts', was an ambitious project – a full-length book for which she hoped to find a publisher; the other, 'The Marigny Case', was almost empty.

Already it was dark enough to light oil-lamps. The

cottage had no electricity. She made the tea and sat down at the kitchen table with the *Jersey Evening Post*.

To her disappointment, there was nothing about Marigny; no one else had come forward with sightings. But, as she flicked through the paper, the name of Claude Yves caught her eye.

The item was headlined 'HUNT FOR BUREAU CHIEF'S SON'. Richard Crozier? That must be George's grandson. Miss Irefield had met him once at George's flat. A scruffy boy, she remembered, who bore little resemblance to the passport snapshot the *Post* had printed.

It seemed that Richard had run away the night before last. It was possible that he might be on the mainland. Yves, while sympathizing fully with the anguish of Mr and Mrs Crozier, expressed the hope that police efforts to trace him were no more thorough than they would have been if Richard's father had not been a policeman himself.

George must be upset: Miss Irefield knew that he was fond of the boy. For an instant she wondered if she should drive into the village and phone him from the public callbox.

Wiser counsels prevailed. How could she help? She had arranged to phone George in the morning; she would talk to him then. Besides, she had more important things to do. She had promised herself a long evening's work trawling through her latest batch of library books. All of them related to the German Occupation of the island.

Her work came before everything else. Somehow she had to find out more about Patrice Marigny.

'You're going there tonight?' Mrs Arkwright said.

It was more of an order than a question.

'Oh, all right.' Winston Arkwright hoped he sounded more convinced than he felt.

'It's in the middle of nowhere. And just one old woman. It's a piece of cake.'

Arkwright stood up. He hated this mean little rented flat. Even the chairs were uncomfortable. He looked down at his mother, who was sitting on the sofa with her cane propped up beside her. All his doubts came to the surface.

'You're sure we've got it right? This is the place to look?'

'It must be. The family went there every summer before the war. I remember the old man talking about it. Mary Rose was the daughter of a farmer who lived in the village.'

'What happened to it in the war?'

'Tillersland let an old couple live there – relatives of the farmer, I think. The Germans turfed them out near the end when they fortified the cliffs.'

Arkwright had wandered across to the window. On the other side was a balcony, still wet after the rain. He stared out across the bay.

'It's going to be a windy night,' he said.

'All the better for you,' his mother said heartlessly.

'I wish we could be certain it was still there,' he said suddenly. 'It's a hell of an assumption to make.'

'We'd have heard if anyone had found it. A van Gogh is news. And it's not the sort of thing that George Crozier would stuff under his mattress.'

'But it's over forty years – '

'Oh, stop whingeing, Winston.' Mrs Arkwright rapped the floor with her cane. 'We've gone over that. Your dad was sure Tillersland hid *The Butcher* on the island. The letter he left for David hints that he left it at Elizabeth Cottage. No one else has found it, have they? According to you, the cottage hasn't even been modernized – why, it's possible that some of the old furniture's still there. It looks good, Winston. And if you had half your father's guts, there'd be no holding you.'

Arkwright sighed. 'I'm just pointing out that it's not *quite* as cut and dried as you seem to think.'

'Don't strike poses at me,' she snapped. 'You're not on stage now. Besides, there's no danger. Even if the worst happens, the coppers won't interfere. And if the old bag sees you, you know what she'll think . . .'

Her voice trailed into silence. Arkwright looked curiously at her.

'What is it?' he asked.

Her wrinkles deepened as she smiled. 'Just an idea. Maybe she *should* see you. What do you think of that?'

Richard Crozier told himself that he was happier than he had been for ages. For the first time in his life he was free. No one could bother him. He could do exactly as he wanted. He must be happy.

It was cold down here. The concrete walls were moist. Even his sleeping-bag felt damp. It wasn't so bad in the daytime – if he crouched outside on the steps, he had enough light to paint or read. There was no risk of anyone surprising him. There were trees all around and he would have plenty of warning if anyone plunged off the path and into the undergrowth.

He drew the sleeping-bag more tightly around him and tried to ignore the fact that he needed to empty his bladder.

No – it was worse at night, when the darkness drove him inside. The door was solid enough, despite the rust; it even had a working bolt. Yesterday he had blocked the loopholes so that it was safe to use a light. He was saving the torch for emergencies. He rationed himself to a single candle.

The worst thing about the night was not the darkness but the noises. As the sun went down, the copse came alive with rustles. It was like a secret city of animals. Last night he had been convinced that something was inside with him. Whatever it was scuttled through the dead leaves on the concrete floor. A mouse? A rat?

Or maybe something even less substantial – the ghost of one of the men who must have shivered here over forty years ago?

The pressure on his bladder was becoming more insistent.

The tubular steel frame of the triple-decker bunk filled the whole of one wall. Originally there had been webbing at each layer – most of that had rotted away. Richard wondered whether they had slept directly on the webbing or on mattresses. The man who used the middle bunk had scratched a mildly pornographic drawing of a woman on the wall beside his head. He had dug deep into the concrete so that his woman survived even when the paint had flaked away from the walls.

On the first night, Richard had stolen some planks from the old woman's garage. 'Stolen' was the wrong word: the planks were more his than hers. He cleaned the frame – removing an entire colony of spiders, alive and dead – and arranged the planks into a precarious slatted shelf on the lowest tier of the bunks. It did not make a comfortable bed, but, sooner or later, he supposed, his body would get used to it.

Sooner or later?

That was the real problem – the one that wouldn't go away. He couldn't stay here for ever, heating tinned food on the Calor gas camping stove and fetching water from the well in the garden of Elizabeth Cottage. Money wasn't the immediate problem. It was more the risk of being recognized if he went into a shop.

But even if he solved the difficulty of supplies, he couldn't spend the rest of his life here. When he had left home, forty-eight hours before, he hadn't really thought beyond the first night. By now he was noticing the drawbacks; he would have given almost anything, for example, for a long soak in a hot bath. He should have followed Bergerac's advice and thought out the consequences of his decision more carefully. At the time, the need to get away had swamped every other consideration.

He could no longer defer getting up. He wriggled out of

the sleeping-bag and stuffed his feet into his shoes. No need to pull on his jersey and jeans – he hadn't taken them off since leaving home.

The door opened quietly – he had borrowed a can of oil from the garage, along with the planks. He tiptoed up the steps.

A gust of wind ruffled his hair. The trees were swaying. The moon was nearly full, but its light was partly obscured by a procession of fast-moving clouds.

It was much colder outside. Richard moved a few paces away from the head of the steps. He could see the yellow glint of oil-light through the trees. Miss Irefield was still up. Last night he had crept up to the uncurtained window and watched as she read and made notes on the kitchen table. Doing that made him feel unpleasantly akin to a spy.

His hand was already on his zip when he heard the crackle of snapping branches, perhaps twenty yards away.

All desire to relieve himself vanished. Could the wind have blown a branch off one of the trees?

A man's voice, muffled and low-pitched, said, 'Oh, bugger!'

Richard held his breath and lowered himself to the ground. A light flashed and died within a single second. A torch?

It wasn't the wind. It wasn't a falling branch.

Someone was coming up the path.

Dampness seeped from the ground into Richard's jeans. It might have been worse: he was downwind of the new arrival. Presumably Miss Irefield had a visitor.

It was odd that the man had come up the path rather than round by the road. But maybe he lived in the village.

Something rustled – probably on the path. It was overhung by branches, some of which had to be pushed aside. Another rustle, farther along – it sounded as if the man was moving in the direction of the cottage.

Richard clasped his hands round his knees. He wouldn't

have long to wait. He would hear the knock on the door, hear it opening and closing. Once the door was shut again and if there was no sound of returning footsteps, it would be safe for him to have a pee and get back inside.

But it didn't work out like that.

The rustling stopped.

After that the only sounds were made by the wind and by Richard's breathing. He waited for what seemed like hours, straining to distinguish the man's movements from the innocent noises of the night.

But no one knocked on the door of Elizabeth Cottage.

Miss Irefield was at peace with herself.

The glow of the lamp cast a charmed circle of light around her. The door of the stove was open and she could feel its warmth on her face. Working in the kitchen was a luxury, but she considered it reasonable in view of the sudden drop in temperature.

Her nib scratched against the paper. Occasionally she turned over a page. Not much had changed in nearly forty years: she might almost have been back in her room at Girton.

At one time she had hoped to spend the rest of her life at Cambridge. Even at school she had known that she was a natural scholar. But her father's last illness in the middle of her third year had changed all that. She had been forced to come down without a degree and spend six precious months nursing him. He had died slowly, painfully and expensively. Only then had the solicitor told her that her father had nothing to leave her but his debts. There was no question of her being able to return to Cambridge.

She had gravitated to London, taught herself shorthand and typing and spent over thirty years in a variety of secretarial jobs. The last of them had been at the *Psychic Review*, where the editor had encouraged her to use her scholarly skills, albeit in a different field.

At first parapsychology had seemed a valueless pseudo-science to her; then it had fascinated her; finally she had realized that she had found her life's work at last. She handed in her notice as a secretary and devoted her energies to research. Alexandra Irefield was a scholar again.

She glanced back through her notes. The sloppiness of other writers infuriated her. Some of them failed to quote their sources. One of the library books even lacked an index. Still, she now had a fair idea of Marigny's career on Jersey, an outline of his exploits with the *Milice* in Vichy France and a sketchy chronology of his life before the war.

Not a nice man: she had established that beyond doubt. She needed to get back to the primary sources – in particular to the diary of Kurt Nullhausen, Marigny's deputy in the Gestapo.

The photograph of Marigny in the *Post* had been taken from a plate in one of the library books. She studied the original. She would give five years of her life in exchange for a good sighting – preferably authenticated by independent witnesses.

Her interest in Marigny was not purely scientific. Miss Irefield was shrewd enough to know that all ghosts are not equal: some have more news value than others. The ghost of a well-documented war criminal, missing since 1945, would be a splendid weapon in the campaign to establish parapsychology in the public mind as a proper subject for research.

The pen moved smoothly across the surface of the paper, leaving behind a neatly disciplined trail of information. Miss Irefield's mind worked with the efficiency of a huge and perfectly designed machine – ingesting, sorting, collating and selecting. Yet part of her was elsewhere, indulging in a fantasy that over the years had become as familiar as her own face and as comforting as an emotional hot-water bottle.

She was in the Senate House at Cambridge. Before an

admiring audience of her intellectual peers, Miss Irefield was receiving a doctorate from the Vice-Chancellor of the university. *Honoris causa.* For services to science.

Her concentration was broken by a tapping on the uncurtained window – the one that faced the seaward side of the house.

She looked up with a start. The pen fell from her hand, rolled across the table and fell to the floor.

A man was standing outside, close enough to the window to be visible against the surrounding darkness. He wore a hat and a coat with an upturned collar. A match flared as he lit a cigarette, casting a flare of light across his features. The pose was a familiar one. Miss Irefield glanced down at the photograph.

She stood up so suddenly that her chair fell backwards on to the floor. Her knees were shaking. She kept her hands on the table to prevent herself from falling.

I must not faint.

The man was Patrice Marigny.

CHAPTER
13

Alice Crozier was no coward. But after she had rung the doorbell, she was sorely tempted to run away.

She was actually turning to go when the door opened. Bergerac had the hint of a smile on his face. She wondered if he had guessed her intention.

'Alice – come in.'

He held the door wide. Before she knew it, she was inside. She had hoped for a brief, businesslike interview at Bergerac's flat, preferably on the doorstep. Instead she had been forced to trail round to the house where he lived for most of the time with Susan Young. Fate wasn't going to make this easy.

'This is a nice surprise,' he said.

She lingered in the hall, resisting his movement to take her coat and wondering if he was being sarcastic.

'They told me at the Bureau you'd be here,' she said. 'I did try phoning but the line was engaged. I hope I haven't disturbed you.'

'No – I'm waiting up for Sue. She's wining and dining a client tonight.'

'I wondered if you'd seen Barney.'

Her voice was meant to be casual, even amused – *Oops, I've temporarily mislaid my husband*. But somehow the words came out with a tremor. And it was galling – not only to have to admit her worry, but also to have to admit it to Jim Bergerac.

'Not since this afternoon,' Bergerac said. 'Anything wrong?'

'I don't know. I thought you might have seen him. I mean, in a funny way you're probably the closest friend he's got.' She listened to herself, aghast, as her control cracked and the words poured out. 'I can't imagine what he thinks he's doing. Now of all times – I've been so worried – it's just – '

Suddenly and humiliatingly she found that she was crying.

Bergerac took her arm and steered her into the sitting-room. All the while he was talking, as if it was perfectly normal for an uninvited guest to arrive at midnight and burst into a flood of tears.

'That chair's the most comfortable. It's a shame that Sue's out. Paper handkerchiefs on that table. Would you like a drink? Or some tea?'

She shook her head and dabbed her eyes with a tissue.

'Oh, dear,' she said between snuffles. 'I feel such a fool.'

'What's happened?'

'First, there's all the worry about Richard – there's still no news. And Barney's taking it badly. He's been drinking a lot, which is most unlike him. And tonight he hasn't come home.'

'What's he doing? Working?'

Alice swallowed and tried to get control of herself. 'No – apparently he left the Bureau at 5.30. He *always* phones when he's going to be late. I've been sitting at home all evening, waiting for him to ring. Clare's staying with friends, thank God. But Barney hasn't phoned. He isn't with George – I've tried that. I just can't understand it.'

'So what are you saying, Alice? That Barney's disappeared too?'

It isn't working!

Damn it, the old woman should have fainted by now – or screamed – or showed some signs of shock. Instead she was leaning across the table staring at him. Jesus, those devouring eyes of hers should have belonged to a real ghost.

Arkwright twisted his face into a sneer. It was the same expression that he had used when he played a wicked sister in a provincial *Cinderella*. He hoped it would be more effective now than it had been then.

Miss Irefield held up one hand in a gesture that might have been designed to beckon him or to ward him off. Her lips moved soundlessly on the other side of the glass dividing them.

Suddenly she darted away from the table and, glancing back at him over her shoulder, ran into the next room. At last she was showing some reaction. Seconds later she reappeared. She had something black in her hands. She was fumbling at it with desperate fingers while keeping her eyes on the window. A second later Arkwright realized what she was holding.

A camera. With a flash attached.

He backed away from the window, finally acknowledging the defeat. The garden path led up to the gate through which he had come. He had no choice but to make a run for it.

The moon slid behind a cloud. The sea roared below him. Damn the Irefield woman – and damn his mother for dreaming up this cock-eyed scheme.

Then he received his second shock of the evening – worse than the first because it was so completely unexpected.

Footsteps on the path on the far side of the garden fence. The click of the latch on the gate.

Who the hell – ?

From the house came a *scrape* and a *clunk*. He knew instantly what it was: the drawing back of a bolt. Sweet Jesus, the old cow was coming after him with her camera at the ready.

Arkwright lost his head. Dropping the cigarette, he ran blindly in the opposite direction to the one from which he had come. He hurled himself round the corner of the house, past the lean-to garage and down the garden towards the sea. He dimly remembered noticing a second gate down here, giving on to the patch of waste land at the top of the cliffs.

The door of Elizabeth Cottage opened with a screech.

The lighted window had destroyed most of his night vision. Now the moon was gone, he had nothing to guide him. He ran into a tree and screamed as the branches poked at his eyes. He tripped over something, which fell with a metallic clatter – a wheelbarrow?

'Monsieur Marigny! Monsieur Marigny! I am your friend!'

Miss Irefield must be off her rocker. Her high, firm voice carried over the background noise of the wind and the sea. Who would believe she'd try to be friendly with a ghost? *Totally fearless – totally mad.* Their positions were now reversed.

Arkwright ran full tilt into the fence. Left or right? He had long since lost the path. There were footsteps behind him – but he couldn't distinguish whether they belonged to one person or to two.

There was a flash behind him – dwarfed into insignificance by the immense darkness of the night.

'Monsieur Marigny – do not be afraid.'

He darted away from that terrible voice, following the line of the fence. In a few yards he blundered into the gate. He tried to unlatch it, but could not find the catch. Instead he plunged over the gate, head first, ripping his mackintosh. His face collided with the rough, wet grass of the cliff-top.

There was another flash.

The old woman was too far away, he thought in a sudden moment of clarity; in any case, his face was turned away from her. He could run round the outside of the fence and reach the cover of the copse.

Beside him someone sneezed.

A third witness – ?

Now there was no more time for thought and only one direction in which to run – downwards, towards the sea. Sobbing with exhaustion, Arkwright stumbled on. The sea was louder here – a monster sucking and pawing at the rocks.

The rocks?

'Monsieur Marigny. *Restez là, je vous en prie!*'

He remembered the surroundings from his reconnaissance by daylight. A drop of perhaps forty feet – a steeply sloping bank of rocky serrations leading down to the sea. A drop that would slash you to death and then drown your remains.

Arkwright fell to the ground. He stretched out his hand. His fingers touched emptiness.

The footsteps were almost on top of him.

'Monsieur Marigny!'

The voice was still high, but now it had another, unexpected note – a girlish enthusiasm, which was profoundly shocking.

Arkwright withdrew his hand. His panic ebbed, leaving a quiet and familiar despair behind. It was all over. He had failed. His face was wet with rain or sea spray. Sometimes you knew that a play had failed in the middle of the first act on the first night. Now he felt the same despair but intensified beyond belief.

Wearily, he sat up and looked round.

There was a third flash.

Barney Crozier wasn't hiding from anyone except himself.

Bergerac tracked him down in twenty minutes by the simple expedient of phoning round the St Helier nightclubs and bars that had extensions to their licences.

Lil's Place was the eighth on his list. Diamanté Lil herself picked up the phone.

'Well, thank God you called,' she said. 'I was just about

to ring you. Barney's sitting by himself at table twenty-three and he's just ordered his own bottle of whisky because the service is so bad.'

'I'll be round in five minutes.' Bergerac rang off.

'I'm coming too,' Alice said.

To all outward appearances, she was back in control again. She had repaired her make-up and was sitting with a straight back on a sofa that was designed for sprawling.

'He's had a few,' Bergerac said. 'Let me go.'

'Don't be ridiculous, Jim. He's my husband.'

'If you go storming in there, it's not going to look very good, is it?'

'What do you mean?'

'It'll look like a nagging wife coming to drag the erring husband home. If he's feeling pigheaded – and he probably is – he's not going to want to come.'

Alice lifted her chin. 'He's not going to have any choice.'

Bergerac was scribbling a note for Susan. 'Claude Yves is using Lil's Place as his regular watering-hole at present.'

'Then I feel sorry for Lil.'

Bergerac shrugged. 'If you want your names in the paper again, that's your affair. What with Richard and this Marigny business, the Croziers are news. Michelin Man's speciality is bitchy little gossip items. And he doesn't like Barney, either.'

'You . . . you think you can be more discreet?' For the first time her voice was uncertain.

'Probably.' Bergerac grinned at her. 'Before you met Barney, he and I got drunk together once or twice. I've had experience.'

They drove to Lil's Place in two cars. Alice agreed to wait outside in her car. Bergerac walked into the nightclub. Lil hurried over to him.

'He's over there,' she said. 'He says he's going to make a formal complaint about the poor quality of the entertainment. In fact, he's said it three times, each time a little louder than before.'

'Cool down,' Bergerac murmured. 'No one wants a fuss. Is Yves here?'

She glanced up at him, immediately understanding what he meant. 'I'm afraid so. No love lost?'

'You could say that. Alice Crozier's outside in the car. Can I have a drink – it'll look less obvious.'

Jean-Luc, the head waiter, already had an orange juice waiting for him when they reached the bar. Glass in hand, Bergerac wandered across the nightclub. Yves, who was sitting by himself at a corner table, waved to him.

'It's the boy wonder,' the reporter said. He was drunk but still in control of himself. 'Looking for recruits?'

'For what?'

'Alcoholics Anonymous.' Yves quaked with laughter. 'I think the Führer over there might want to sign on the dotted line once he's sobered up.'

Crozier was swaying in his chair, beating time with both feet to a Fats Waller number the pianist was playing; he was also tunelessly and audibly whistling along with the music.

'Happy as a sandboy, eh? Lil would have had him chucked out hours ago if he wasn't a copper. Afraid to touch him.'

Bergerac pulled out a chair and sat down beside Yves. There wasn't much time. When Barney got really drunk in the old days, one of two things happened: either he collapsed in a maudlin heap or he went berserk. By the look of him, he was on the brink of doing one or the other.

'I wonder what he's celebrating,' Yves said in a dreamy voice. 'It's almost worth getting hold of a photographer.'

'Claude,' Bergerac said gently, 'let me tell your fortune. If this gets into the press, whether it's under your name or someone else's, several things are going to happen. First, no one in the States Police is ever going to talk to you again.'

Yves blew a raspberry. 'No one in the Bureau talks to me in any case. That's Crozier's doing. That Marigny story really upset him.'

'If this gets out, no one else will talk to you either.'

Both men looked up as Crozier knocked over one of the empty chairs at his table. Barney was nearly over the brink.

'Is this blackmail, Sergeant?' Yves inquired. 'An unlawful attempt to muzzle the press?'

'Be your age, Claude. Telling the truth is one thing, but being malicious is something else. Barney's under a lot of stress right now.'

'You must allow me to be the best judge of that.'

'Most of your income is from Jersey papers, isn't it, Claude?'

'What's that got to do with it?'

'Local editors and the States Police have a very cooperative relationship.'

Yves played with his glass. 'You . . . you wouldn't dare.'

'And one more thing,' Bergerac said. 'You're driving yourself tonight, aren't you? I suppose a car's vital for your job. Be a bit awkward if you didn't have a valid driving licence.'

'I might use a taxi tonight, actually.'

'And every night? And every day?'

There was a long silence. Finally Yves sighed.

'You drive a hard bargain.' His voice was almost affectionate. 'I thought this was too good to be true.'

Bergerac stood up. 'I'll let you know if anything comes up. Barney's not the sort to bear grudges.'

'First the stick, then the carrot?'

'You got it, Claude.'

Bergerac made his way over to Crozier. The level in the bottle had sunk below the half-way mark. The Chief

Inspector had lost his interest in music. His body slumped in his chair. A few more inches and he would be under the table. He stared at Bergerac and blinked.

'Hello, Jim.' He hauled himself up in the chair and pushed the bottle across the table. 'Have a drink. It's on me.'

Bergerac held up his untouched glass. 'I've got one, thanks.'

'Have a real drink. I know you don't, but make an exception, just for once. Just for Barney, eh? Exceptional circumstances call for exceptional actions. Special duties. Have a drink. That's an order, Sergeant.'

'Been here long?' Bergerac picked up the bottle, more to keep it away from Crozier than for any other reason.

Crozier frowned. 'A while. I was somewhere else before this. And somewhere else before that. You know how it is. Do you remember that night just after we had the results of our sergeant's exams? Now *that* was a night to remember. Where did we go then? It's funny, I can't remember. Funny!'

Bergerac grinned. Crozier roared with laughter.

'I can't remember either,' Bergerac said. 'We have to go somewhere else now.'

'Do we?'

'Don't you remember?'

'Can't say I do. But I expect you're right. Let's go. This place is so *dull*. DULL!'

'Sh, Barney. You'll hurt their feelings.'

'Good point, Jim. You're no fool, you know that? No need to hurt people's feelings unnecessarily. Too many hurt feelings in this world already. It's not good. Let's drink to that.'

'We'd better hurry.' Bergerac stood up, still holding the bottle. 'We're late.'

'All right.' Crozier swallowed the rest of the whisky in his glass and stood up, holding on to the table. 'Whoops!

You'll bring the bottle, of course? We might need a little refreshment on the way. Plan ahead, that's my motto.'

Jean-Luc was hovering. Bergerac beckoned him. The waiter came round to Crozier's other side. Lil had shrewdly provided a diversion for the rest of her clientele by bringing forward the rock band and the light-show that had been scheduled for later in the evening. They managed to get Crozier into the foyer with remarkably little disturbance.

'I hate that music,' Crozier said. 'Richard listens to it all the time, you know. Richard.'

His face began to break up.

At a nod from Bergerac, Jean-Luc edged away.

'Come on, Barney.' Bergerac tightened his hold on Crozier's arm. 'Alice's waiting outside in the car.'

Miss Irefield wound on the film and fell to her knees.

'You *are* Patrice Marigny, aren't you?'

She had never dreamed that it would be like this. Her own courage did not amaze her; she had always taken it for granted that she was brave – like the colour of one's eyes, it was something one was born with. It seemed to her that the darkness had turned the cliff-top into a windswept confessional. She waited on tenterhooks for an answer.

All she heard was a stifled groan.

'Monsieur Marigny?' she tried again. She swept her free arm in an arc. There was nothing there, of course. Nothing that a hand of flesh and blood could touch.

The dampness soaked unnoticed through the knees of her thick woollen tights. She shuffled forward with her hand outstretched.

'I am your friend, Monsieur,' she said coaxingly. '*Je suis votre amie.*'

Then she felt a blow between her shoulder-blades. She was falling forward. The palms of her hands grated against rock and turned to fire. The precious camera was gone.

It was the loss of the camera that made her scream.

CHAPTER
14

George Crozier looked small and forlorn beside the bulk of the desk sergeant in reception.

Bergerac came out as soon as he heard the old man was there. George's face brightened as he appeared.

'Sorry to trouble you again, Jim. I thought Barney was here.'

'He phoned in sick this morning,' Bergerac said. 'Or rather, Alice did. She reckoned he'd be back tomorrow.'

'What's up with him?'

'Upset stomach. And Alice says he's feeling rotten generally.'

It was an accurate if misleading description of Crozier's hangover.

George shook his head. 'They're having a rough time, those two.'

'Anyway – is there something I can do?'

'Well, it's two things, really. But I'm sure you're busy. Not really important.'

Bergerac glanced at his watch. 'I have a tea-break at three o'clock,' he lied. 'Come up to the canteen and have a cup with me.'

He found a table in the smoking section of the room so George could smoke his pipe. The tea came in white, half-pint mugs. Everyone drank it sweet because it was undrinkable without sugar.

George spluttered after his first mouthful. 'We used to run tanks on stuff like this.'

Bergerac pushed the sugar towards him. 'What's on your mind?'

'Alex – Miss Irefield. She didn't phone me this morning. She said she would.'

'Maybe she changed her mind.'

George shook his head. 'You don't understand. If Alex says she'll do something, that's it. It's done. We were going to arrange a meeting – she wants to bring me up to date on Marigny – she's been doing some research on him, you see. And I was going to show her Marie's painting.'

'You tried phoning her?'

'The cottage isn't on the phone. And Jim – there's another reason I wanted a word with her. Because of Richard.' The old man hesitated. 'Don't get me wrong – but what if he's still on the island?'

Bergerac concealed his impatience. 'It's not a big place. We've checked everywhere he might have gone. We've talked to his friends – even the ones that Alice and Barney didn't know he had.'

'Sure – I wasn't trying to teach you your job. It's just I wondered if you'd tried the cottage.'

'You think we should? Surely Miss Irefield would let you know if he turned up there?'

George dug the ashes out of his pipe with a used match. 'She might not see him. Not if he was around the cottage rather than in it. The point is, Richard used to love it. When the kids were younger, Barney and Alice had a few holidays there. That was before Alex moved in. I took him there myself once or twice – for picnics and such. It's a good place for kids – there's the garden and the land around the cliffs; it all belongs to the cottage. You can get down to the sea. There's a little wood you can camp in. There are caves and some ruined farm buildings. There's even an old German bunker, slap in the middle of the wood.' He filled the pipe with trembling fingers. 'These last few years he lost interest in the place. It's natural enough.

When kids get to a certain age, they want the bright lights, they want to be with their friends.'

'Even so, you think Richard might be hiding up there?'

'It's possible. He's like his dad, you see.'

'Eh?'

'When Barney gets upset, really upset, he doesn't want company. He doesn't go to his friends. He doesn't want to talk about it if he can help it. He wants to lick his wounds by himself. Haven't you noticed?'

Bergerac shook his head. A nightclub wasn't the obvious place for a person who wanted to be alone. Then he remembered how Barney had been last night: by himself at a table with a bottle for company. Maybe he'd looked for privacy in a crowd. True, Barney had welcomed Bergerac; but that was partly chance and partly because his alcohol content had passed a certain point. He could just as easily have thrown a punch at him.

'Well?' George was looking anxiously across the table. 'Can you do anything?'

There was a slight and probably unconscious stress on the *you*. In theory, all Bergerac had to do was lift up a phone and ask a constable to visit Elizabeth Cottage; anyone on the force could have a word with Miss Irefield and take a look around.

In practice, it wasn't so easy. George wasn't talking to him as a policeman but as a friend – as a friend of the whole family. It was truer than George knew; in the last few days, Bergerac had lent a sympathetic ear to three generations of Croziers. There was no escaping it. This was personal.

'Tell you what,' Bergerac said. 'I'll drive over after work. I'll have a look round and I'll get Miss Irefield to phone you.'

George's face lost its worried look. 'You're a good lad, Jim. I knew you would.'

*

Peggy Masters waylaid Bergerac on his way back from the canteen. She was waving a flimsy sheet of paper from the teleprinter. She seemed to have picked up George's worried expression.

'Should we do something about this? It's just come in for the Chief Inspector.'

Bergerac took the message. It was highly confidential; messages from Special Branch always were.

His eyebrows rose when he saw the date on it. 'Taken their time, haven't they? We should have had this forty-eight hours ago.'

Peggy pursed her lips and nodded. 'It doesn't surprise me.'

It was an article of faith with her that no other police department in the country approached the efficiency of the Bureau des Etrangers.

'He's probably moved on by now.' Bergerac shrugged. 'I suppose we'd better check it out.'

He glanced round the office and decided that Detective Constable Wilson was, by a short head, less overworked than anyone else.

'Terry – here's a little job for you.'

Wilson looked up from his typewriter. 'Jim, I've got to get out three – '

'It can wait. Ever heard of Yosef Dulov?'

'Israeli, isn't he? Sort of freelance Nazi-hunter?'

'That's the one. Combines vengeance with the profit motive. The Israelis have disowned him, and so has the Simon Wiesenthal Centre. Special Branch think he flew into Jersey from Bristol – two days ago.'

'Two days? But – '

'I know – now they tell us. Apparently they were looking for someone else and it took time to make the identification. He's travelling with an American passport, they think, under the name of Jerome Fisher.'

'A fisher of men? Get it?'

Terry Wilson had a tendency to crack obvious jokes. Bergerac had a tendency to ignore them.

'Look into it, will you? He's probably gone, but you never know.'

'We haven't any Nazis here, have we?'

'Not that I know of. But we do have a lot of banks. Dulov's meant to be a wealthy man.'

Wilson leant back and scratched his beard. He was a huge man – taller than Bergerac and much heavier.

'We don't want to collar him?' he asked.

Bergerac shook his head. 'He doesn't break our laws, not that I know of. Just keep tabs on him. If you can find him.'

'Jim!' It was Peggy, calling across the office.

He looked up. She pointed at the telephone.

'It's that man Dulov again. Now Interpol would like a word.'

'You panicked,' Mrs Arkwright said. 'That's the long and the short of it.'

'For God's sake, Mother! I was lucky to escape in one piece.'

She sniffed. 'I reckon you made most of it up, Winston. You always were a good liar.'

'I'm *not* lying. It was all your fault, in any case. You said the Irefield woman would scream blue murder and go into palpitations when she saw me. Well, you were wrong. *She* came after *me*. And two other people were up there – at least two.'

'And what do you think they were doing?' she snarled. 'Getting a breath of fresh air?'

'I don't know.' Arkwright shuddered. 'That was the worst of it, in a way. It was all so confusing and so dark. That bloody woman trying to make friends with a ghost. Someone screamed and I just ran. Honestly, Mother, I'm lucky to be alive. I could have gone over that cliff.'

'You should have got the camera.'

'How could I do that?'

She shrugged, tacitly conceding the point. 'It could have been worse, I suppose. Irefield will think she's got a snapshot of a ghost. That's something.'

There was a long silence. The rain beat against the window-pane. The grey sea merged imperceptibly with the grey sky. It was all going wrong, Winston Arkwright thought. What a dreary island this was. He should never have allowed his mother to talk him into coming. It wasn't fair.

His mother clicked her tongue against her false teeth. 'Suppose you're right,' she said slowly. 'Suppose there were two other people out there. Could they be after the van Gogh? No, that won't work. No one else has seen the letter. A couple of lovers, maybe?'

'No,' Arkwright said. 'It wasn't like that.'

'Read me the letter again,' she commanded.

Arkwright picked it up from the table. By now he could almost have recited it by heart.

'"My dear David,"' he began. '"If you get this letter, it is probable that I shall be dead. Marie Crozier will give it to you if it's humanly possible to do so. She and Elsie have been so good to me these last few years. First, and most important, I want you to know how much you have meant to me. It is never easy to say these things face to face – "'

'Skip the sob-stuff,' Mrs Arkwright said harshly. 'It's the chunk at the end that counts.'

'"I'm afraid there won't be as much money as I had hoped, partly because of this dreadful war. As you know, much of my income comes from an annuity which will not survive me. There is a little over a thousand pounds on deposit at the bank. You will also inherit a number of shares – though God knows what their post-war value will be, if any. The house, of course, is rented. You'll have the contents, naturally, and the freehold of the cottage. Do not, I beg you, dispose of the cottage. It would be most unwise.

'"We had so many happy times there when you were young and your mother was alive. It was she who persuaded me to buy it. I often think of the games you used to play there – do you remember? With Sidney and Mary Rose? When you were smugglers hiding from the customs officers – I shall always remember that. The officers never found the contraband in your secret cache. It was curious how memory, after the event, allocates value to some moments and not to others. A mysterious process, indeed. But it is getting late and – "'

'We don't need the rest,' Mrs Arkwright interrupted. 'Sentimental old goat, wasn't he? It's all perfectly clear.'

'But is it?' Arkwright threw down the letter and ran his fingers through his thinning hair. 'You don't think we're reading too much into it?'

She shook her head. 'It's his last letter to his son, who he hasn't seen for years. He's talking about his assets. Why doesn't he even mention the van Gogh, the biggest asset of the lot? And all that guff about the cottage – "Do not, I beg you, dispose of the cottage" – why not, for God's sake, unless the van Gogh was there? It's a pound to a penny that David would have known exactly where he meant by "your secret cache".'

'Sidney and Mary Rose?'

'Sid was the farmer's son – he died at Dunkirk. His sister Mary Rose was killed in a car crash before the war. We'll get no answers from them.' Mrs Arkwright cackled unexpectedly. 'Unless the Irefield woman has got a hot-line to heaven.'

'It's no use.' Arkwright lit a cigarette and wondered if it was too soon to have a drink. 'Look – why don't we cut our losses and get back to London?'

'Now?' his mother flared up. 'Are you mad? Pull yourself together, Winston. There's nothing to worry about. All we need is to get Irefield out of the cottage for a few hours.'

Arkwright closed his eyes. 'I am not going back there alone. That's final.'

'No, you're not,' his mother agreed. 'You'd run away if you saw your own shadow. That's why I'm coming with you.'

It was still raining when Bergerac edged the Triumph Roadster into the narrow road that led up to the cottage.

The light was already beginning to fade. It was nearly six o'clock. He had been delayed by the Dulov business. Interpol was breathing heavily down his neck. The Spanish police had phoned. Special Branch had suddenly revised its opinion of the relative unimportance of Jerome Fisher. A routine inquiry had turned into a murder hunt. Crozier would have a fit when he heard what had been happening in his absence.

The road meandered upwards between high hedges. The surface was pitted with pot-holes.

According to Terry Wilson, Jerome Fisher had come through immigration at the airport and vanished into thin air. He hadn't hired a car. He hadn't gone to a hotel. Most importantly of all, there was no record of him leaving the island.

In other words, the responsibility for tracing him rested fairly and squarely on the Bureau.

The lane levelled out. The hedges dropped away on either side. Finally the tarmac petered out into rough grass. Bergerac braked and switched off the engine.

On his right was a low fence, beyond which a scruffy garden sloped down to Elizabeth Cottage. To his left a muddy path crossed the grass and disappeared into a wilderness of young trees and scrubby bushes; that must be the shortcut to the village. The rain drummed on the hood of the car. Bergerac realized that he had left both his coat and his umbrella at the Bureau.

Cursing, he got out of the car and turned up the collar of

his leather jacket. He opened the gate and ran down the path to the door of the cottage. He knocked sharply on it.

'Come on!' he muttered as the seconds dragged by.

The door remained closed.

He knocked again and edged along the wall of the cottage to the nearest window. He put his face close to the glass and stared in. He was looking at an old-fashioned kitchen with a range on the gable wall. In the middle was a heavy pine table, littered with books and papers. The door to the adjoining room was ajar. He could see the corner of the bookcase. He craned his head for a better view.

It was then that he saw the overturned chair.

There was probably a perfectly simple explanation. Nevertheless, Bergerac sprinted back to the door and tried the handle.

The door opened with a screech of wood on stone. He stood for a moment, trying to get his bearings. The kitchen was cold and smelled musty. The range was out.

'Miss Irefield? This is Jim Bergerac, States Police.'

There was no reply.

'Miss Irefield?'

He took a step forward. The face of Patrice Marigny stared up at him from the table. He poked the pile of notes with his forefinger. Marigny. The Gestapo. The Occupation of Jersey. The notes were in a neat, upright hand. The last thing she had written was: *Consult Nullhausen's journal. Location? Query: is he –*

The sentence ended in a spatter of ink-blots. But where was the fountain-pen? Bergerac glanced under the table. The black, old-fashioned pen had rolled against one of the legs. Its gold nib gave off a faint gleam. Miss Irefield was not the sort of person who would forget to cap her pen when she had finished using it. Nor would she leave it on the floor.

Bergerac quickly searched the rest of the cottage. The sitting-room with all its books was a cheerless place, facing north; no doubt she used the kitchen because it was warmer. He found no obvious signs of disturbance. There was a small, primitive bathroom tacked on to the kitchen; on the window-sill was a single toothbrush with worn grey bristles.

A door in the kitchen led to a narrow, boxed-in staircase. On the upper floor were two small bedrooms containing more books and the minimum of furniture. The room that Miss Irefield used had a high single bed covered with a purple eiderdown. The wallpaper was sprinkled with faded roses.

The cottage could have been charming, but the overall effect was one of unloved dinginess. It was not a home. It was a place where someone worked, ate and slept.

Next he checked the garage. It was unlocked. The Morris Minor was still inside. Fifty years of rubbish was stacked around the walls. Bergerac tapped the bonnet of the car; nowadays Morris Minors were desirable motors – almost collectors' pieces. An ominous patch of rust was spreading along the nearside wing from the headlight. He prodded it experimentally. It needed attention badly.

He had found nothing that should disturb him as a policeman. A lot of older people in country areas rarely bothered to lock their doors. A chair and a pen out of place? Maybe Miss Irefield had other things on her mind; maybe she left in a hurry. The car in the garage? Well, a friend might have picked her up or she could have walked to the village.

Then why did he feel so uneasy?

Suddenly the light in the garage diminished.

Bergerac had heard nothing and seen nothing. But he knew that someone was behind him.

He swung round. Richard Crozier was standing in the doorway. His clothes were filthy. There were dark smudges beneath his eyes and his hair was lank with grease.

'Mr Bergerac.' The boy's voice was surprisingly calm.

'Well, I'm – '

Richard stopped him with a wave of his hand. 'You'd better come quickly. I've just found Miss Irefield. I think she's dead.'

CHAPTER
15

Barney Crozier was pale and angry.

He paced up and down his office. Alice had taken Richard home.

'Why the hell did you phone Yves?' he shouted. 'I thought I'd made it clear that no one in the Bureau was to give him the time of day. Let alone a story. Let alone *this* story.'

The anger, Bergerac guessed, was partly a by-product of relief. If Michelin Man had not been a convenient focus for it, Crozier would have found someone or something else.

'Well?' Crozier banged his desk with the palm of his hand. The shock made him wince.

'Barney – how much do you remember about last night?'

'What's that got to do with it?'

'You had a skinful – and it showed. Yves was there in Lil's Place. He has a grudge against you. He was going to get a photographer in.'

Crozier flushed. He sank into a chair. 'Alice didn't mention that. What happened?'

'Alice didn't know.' Bergerac leant forward. 'To preserve your precious reputation,' he said carefully, 'I threatened to destroy his job and have him done for driving under the influence. I bullied him, Barney, and I don't like bullying people, even for your sake. I also said that if he co-operated, we'd let bygones be bygones. Fair enough?'

'All right, Jim.' The flush receded from Crozier's face. 'I didn't appreciate the full ... Damn it, Jim – I'm sorry. OK?'

'OK.'

'And I'm also grateful you found Richard,' he added ungraciously.

'I think he was going to come in of his own accord. It was just that he saw my car. Anyway, it was your dad's idea that he might be somewhere round the cottage.'

Crozier waved away the disclaimer. 'And Richard tells me you pulled him out of trouble once before. Why didn't you tell me?'

Bergerac shrugged. 'I don't know. He needed another chance.'

'I wish he hadn't found the body.' Crozier caught Bergerac's eye. 'And I don't mean because of the publicity. I was thinking of Richard. It wasn't a good way to see death for the first time.'

Crozier was right. Miss Irefield had fallen head-first over the cliff. The ragged surface of rocks, sloping down to the sea, had slashed her clothes and ripped her skin. At some point in the fall she had bounced and dented her skull; the preliminary examination suggested that it was this wound that had killed her. As the final humiliation, the sea had refused to cover her body and bear it away: instead, her corpse had wedged itself in a crevice at the foot of the cliff, just out of reach of the high-tide mark.

By some freakish chance, her body could be seen from above only if you stood in one place. It was not a dignified sight. Miss Irefield was upside-down. From the top of the cliff you saw two skinny legs, splayed apart at an angle they had never achieved in life; you saw part of her clothing, reduced by rain and sea spray to blackened rags; you saw the few splashes of blood that the water had failed to wash away.

'Accident?' Crozier said. 'Suicide? Murder?'

'Nothing to support the suicide theory. At first I assumed it was an accident: she was working at night – wanted a breath of air – missed her footing. No sign of intruders; no sign of robbery.'

'But Richard's evidence – '

'I know,' Bergerac said wearily. 'He tells the same story, over and over again. Sometime late in the evening, he left the bunker for a pee. He heard a man on the path. He waited, and a bit later there was shouting. He was worried about Miss Irefield, so he moved down to the garden gate on the lane. Visibility's bad, but he thinks the man ran down the path to the other gate, the one which leads on to the cliffs. Miss Irefield ran after him, taking pot-shots with her camera. Richard didn't get a clear view of the man; he was too far away. But he thinks that one of the flashes showed a second man, standing by the cliff gate.'

'He *thinks* this,' Crozier said. 'He *thinks* that. He'd sound great in court. Then what happened?'

'He's not sure. He moved a little way down the path, but he still couldn't see anything, and the wind and sea made it hard to hear. He thinks Miss Irefield was saying something. There was another flash and he saw something light-coloured at the edge of the cliff – maybe a raincoat. He's only certain of one thing, Barney – and that's the scream.'

'Did he think it was hers?'

'Screams can be sexless. He didn't know. We presume it was hers.'

'You'd think he'd have had the sense to get help.'

'Come on, Barney – he's fifteen and scared out of his wits. He ran for cover. Don't tell me you'd have done any different at his age.'

'It was still stupid,' Crozier snapped.

'Everyone can be stupid. He hasn't got a monopoly on that.' Bergerac stared at Crozier until the latter looked away. 'Besides,' he added in a gentler voice, 'he had the courage to come out later. No one was around. The lights were out. He thought Miss Irefield had gone to bed. And in the morning he looked round again. Nothing was out of place. He didn't find the body until just before I arrived.'

'Maybe you're right.' Crozier's voice was grudging. 'Dad said I judge the boy too hard. I don't know.'

Bergerac had had enough of breast-beating Croziers to last him the rest of his life.

'The big question,' he said firmly, 'is whether Dulov's involved. It can't be coincidence.'

Crozier seized on the diversion. 'Are the Spanish police sure about the identification?'

Bergerac nodded. 'Monsieur Vimy of San Sebastian is definitely Patrice Marigny. They matched the dental work and the fingerprints. The Israelis were only too pleased to help. He lived by himself in a small villa outside the town. The daily maid found his body when she turned up for work, nearly two weeks ago. The house had been turned over and a lot of stuff was missing. It looked like a robbery that had gone wrong.'

'The Spanish took their time about identifying him.'

'It wasn't their fault. Vimy had been there for years – they thought he was just another wealthy ex-pat. No – oddly enough they got on to him through Dulov. Dulov left his prints on a door handle. It's the first mistake he's ever made – the first bit of hard evidence he's left behind him.'

'I get it. When they realized they had the prints of a Nazi-hunter, they naturally wondered who was the Nazi?'

Bergerac looked at his watch. The scene-of-the-crime team was up at Elizabeth Cottage. The floodlights were up. The men were searching, measuring, photographing and talking to the neighbours, none of whom lived within 200 yards of the cottage. Bergerac should be up there with them. One vital piece of evidence had yet to be found. Maybe they would need the frogmen for that.

'Well, what's the connection?' Crozier said. 'Dulov kills and robs Marigny in Spain. Nearly a fortnight later, Dad sees a man who he identifies, if that's the word, as the ghost of young Marigny. Miss Irefield wants to investigate the ghost. Dulov flies into Jersey. Miss Irefield falls off a cliff in the company of one or possibly two men. It's not exactly a logical scenario, is it? It doesn't make sense.'

'The profit motive?' Bergerac said.

'Eh?'

'Dulov's family died in the camps, but he traces war criminals at least partly for the money. Maybe Marigny talked before he died – tried to bribe Dulov off by promising him some war loot which was still on Jersey.'

'Sounds a bit thin to me.'

'And maybe he saw that item in the *Post* about your dad seeing Marigny. He could well have connections on Jersey. I don't know. I can't help feeling that if we knew exactly what Marigny was doing in 1945, we'd stand a far better chance of finding out what's happening now.'

'Rubbish!' Crozier said with unexpected vehemence. 'There's no point in poking around in the past. I don't want you squandering your time on that.'

'But Barney – '

There was a tap on the door. Crozier shouted, 'Come!'

Barry Goddard poked his head into the room. 'Terry's just called in. They've found the camera.'

Bergerac stood up. 'I'm on my way.' He glanced down at Crozier. 'There's nothing you can do here tonight. Why don't you go home?'

'When I need your advice on how to conduct this department,' Crozier said, 'I shall ask for it. On your bike, Sergeant.'

A little later the phone began to ring.

Crozier hesitated – wishing he had taken Bergerac's advice and gone home. He picked up the handset.

'Barney, dear.' It was the old, evil voice.

'What do you want?' he said hoarsely.

143

'I've just heard the news – it was on TV. An accident, was it?'

Crozier said nothing.

'Now, don't be difficult, Barney. I'm sure it was an accident. A little slip on a dark night. Remember that.'

'I'm afraid I – '

'And if you forget, someone might remember your mother's little slip.' A thin giggle floated down the line. 'Naughty, naughty Marie.'

It was long after midnight when Bergerac returned from Elizabeth Cottage.

He went into the main office and left the two exhibits on his desk. They were a small return on the evening's work. Exhibit A: a battered 35 mm camera with a broken flash and a leather case stained with sea water; the strap had snagged round a tongue of rock near the bottom of the cliff, otherwise the sea would have ground it to pieces. Bergerac had removed the film and had it biked to headquarters a few hours earlier. Exhibit B: a half-smoked Silk Cut cigarette in an advanced state of disintegration because of the rain; it looked fairly fresh, but it might well have nothing to do with the events of last night.

He dumped the two plastic bags and phoned the technician. He had time to snatch a cup of coffee from the vending machine before he went down to the basement.

The light was on over the dark-room door. In a few seconds the technician joined him.

'Hello, Jim. You want the good news or the bad news first?'

Bergerac looked sourly at him. 'Any news will do.'

The technician shrugged. He was a middle-aged man whose heavy black eyebrows gave him a permanently sinister expression.

'The film wasn't ruined,' he said. 'That's the good news.

144

The bad news is that Miss Irefield wasn't too good with a camera.'

'I knew it,' Bergerac said. 'What have you got?'

There were three black-and-white prints; the rest of the film had not been exposed. The first print was a grey blur of unidentifiable shapes. So was the second.

'She wasn't using the auto-focus,' the technician said unnecessarily. 'The lens's focal length was probably about four to five feet. The subject must have been at least forty feet away. In any case, she didn't realize that the flash's range is limited. But luckily . . .'

He broke off and pushed the third print towards Bergerac. It showed a man crouching on the ground. He wore a mackintosh and a hat. The face was looking up at the camera. It was out of focus but still recognizable.

A long, mobile face that might have belonged to an off-duty clown. A clown who was extremely scared of someone or something.

A clown called Patrice Marigny.

As he walked back upstairs, Bergerac conducted an argument with his conscience.

This was his case, he told himself; Crozier had said nothing to the contrary. It was true that Crozier had been here tonight more as a parent than as a policeman. It was also true that he might assign the case to someone other than Bergerac tomorrow. Given the potential Dulov connection, he might even take it over himself.

Perfectly reasonable – though someone upstairs might raise an eyebrow because of Crozier's personal connection, through George, to Miss Irefield and Elizabeth Cottage.

Bergerac sat down at his desk and stared at the long, sad face of Patrice Marigny. There was a well-established procedure for making appeals through the press. Technically, the decision should be referred to Crozier – and possibly he himself would have to refer it upstairs.

Yet Crozier was acting strangely at present. Getting drunk – totally plastered in public – was completely out of character. It wasn't just Richard's vanishing trick; it went deeper than that. He should have been over the moon this evening; instead he had been angry and worried.

And why was Crozier so set against Bergerac investigating the roots of this business – Marigny's activities in wartime Jersey? It was obvious, at least to Bergerac, that the past was somehow relevant to this case.

Marigny arrested Henry Tillersland. Why? Tillersland killed himself.

Richard had the Tillersland papers temporarily in his possession; Crozier now seemed uninterested in finding out why the boy had taken them.

An old woman phoned Crozier the other day. What had Peggy said? *Private family information* – that was it. *About the Chief Inspector's mother.*

Marie Crozier was dead. Marie Crozier had painted Patrice Marigny. Marie Crozier had worked for Henry Tillersland.

Bergerac sighed. His coffee had cooled to an undrinkable brown liquid.

Take it a little further.

Miss Irefield had died at Elizabeth Cottage. The cottage was owned by Barney's father. George had seen Marigny's ghost outside his flat. On the same evening, George might have had a break-in. After the war, George and Marie Crozier had inherited what was left of Tillersland's assets – including the cottage.

So what was Barney Crozier up to? What was he trying to hide? He couldn't hide the photograph – but he could certainly block its publication, perhaps indefinitely.

The question and the possibilities swirled through Bergerac's mind. He was tired – maybe he wasn't thinking straight. Something was missing.

Dulov? Where the hell did he fit in?

Bergerac rubbed his eyes. Right now, only one question was really important: was Crozier playing a double game?

There was only one way to find out: by forcing Barney's hand.

Bergerac found an envelope for the photograph and picked up his car keys. Before he could change his mind, he drove down to Lil's Place. To his relief he met neither Lil nor Jean-Luc.

On the stage a man and a woman were singing a sugary folk-rock hit from the 1960s. Michelin Man was sitting alone at his usual table. Bergerac shouldered his way through the crowd and sat down beside him.

'Hello, Jim,' Yves wheezed. 'I owe you a drink. I'm celebrating. Irefield will be in the nationals tomorrow.' He rubbed his hands together. 'Ghosts, Gestapo and sudden death. It's a winning formula. What'll you have to drink?'

'Nothing.' Bergerac pulled the photograph out of the envelope. 'This was found in the dead woman's camera.'

'Dear God!' Yves jerked his hand away as though the photo was literally hot to the touch. 'That's Marigny.'

'Or someone who looks like him. Do you want the picture to go with your story?'

'Now wait a moment.' Yves's small, shrewd eyes peeped over the rim of his glass at Bergerac. 'There are channels for this sort of thing. It takes a bit of time. And why just me rather than the press as a whole? Don't get me wrong, but it all smells just a tiny bit iffy to me.'

'Do you want it?' Bergerac said. 'Or not?'

'Look, Jim – what's the story? I need to know more. Off the record, I promise.'

Bergerac shook his head. *I've got a wild idea that the incorruptible Barney Crozier might be involved in some sort of cover-up.* He couldn't say that to Yves. Not to anyone. Suddenly he felt very tired. He slid the photograph back into the envelope.

Michelin Man watched him.

Bergerac pushed back his chair.

'Don't be in such a hurry, Jim,' Yves said. 'Could I attribute it to the Bureau? Or even to you?'

A plump hand with ragged, grubby nails sidled across the table. The fingers stroked the envelope.

'"Police sources",' Bergerac said. 'Something like that. Keep it vague, OK? Don't worry – they won't dare to deny it.'

'It's on your head, Jim.' Yves drew the envelope towards him. 'Sure you won't have that drink? You look as if you could do with it.'

CHAPTER
16

The museum was in a Queen Anne house near Fort Regent. It opened at nine o'clock. Bergerac was on the doorstep by five to.

He rang the doorbell, hammered on the door and waited. He had managed two hours' sleep last night and his face was gaunt with tiredness. Desperation drove him on. By now Crozier would be back in control at the Bureau. A few hours later, the photograph of Marigny's ghost would be published. It might even be out now – Michelin Man was quite capable of trying to sell his scoop to Channel TV.

He rang the bell again, wondering if he was chasing up a blind alley. According to the most scholarly of Miss Irefield's library books, the original of Nullhausen's diary was held by the Channel Islands Historical Trust.

The Trust, Bergerac had discovered, was a private organization funded by industry and by private individuals. It administered several historical buildings in Jersey and maintained a small museum and library in St Helier. It also encouraged the survival of traditional cottage industries by leasing equipment and premises at extremely low rates.

Chains and bolts rattled on the other side of the door. The door opened a crack; it was still on the chain. A portly man in a peaked cap stared indignantly at Bergerac.

'We're not open yet. Can't you read?'

'Police,' Bergerac said wearily.

'*Police?*' The man looked disdainfully at Bergerac's leather jacket. 'I suppose you have some identification?'

149

Bergerac dragged out his warrant card and passed it through the crack. The man studied it, back and front. He held it up to the light. He compared the photograph with the reality before him.

'Look,' Bergerac said. 'I'm in a hurry. This is an official inquiry. I want to see the senior person here.'

'We have to make quite sure. Dr Godly is most insistent about security.'

'You can eat my bloody card if you want to. Just let me in.'

'All right, Sergeant. There's no need for that sort of language.'

A church clock struck nine.

The man opened the door. 'You might as well have waited,' he said triumphantly.

Bergerac pushed past him into the house. 'Where's this Dr Godly?'

'I'm here,' a woman said above his head. 'What's all this racket?'

'I was merely following standing orders, Dr Godly – '

'My name's Bergerac, Dr Godly.' He began to climb the stairs. 'States Police.'

He stopped abruptly. He had been expecting a near relation to Miss Irefield, not a small but shapely blonde in a very short skirt.

'You've come about the diary?' she said. 'Oh, *good*!'

Bergerac blinked. 'How did you know that?'

'Well, why else? The police aren't exactly regular visitors.'

She took his card from his hand.

'The Bureau des Etrangers, eh? A real detective sergeant? We are honoured. We'd better go to my office.'

'Would you mind telling me what you're going on about?' Bergerac said absently; Dr Godly's rear elevation was as distracting as the front.

'The Nullhausen Diary, of course.' She opened a door on

the first landing and ushered him into her room. 'I must say that I'd hoped to hear something sooner. It's a good ten weeks now.'

'Since what?'

'Since it was stolen.' She turned and saw his bewildered face. 'We're at cross purposes, aren't we, Sergeant? Have I been taking too much for granted again?'

'I think we both have. I didn't know it was stolen.'

'Then why . . .' she paused and started again: 'Do sit down. Shall I talk first? The diary was loaned to an exhibition in Paris during the winter. At the Pompidou Centre. The theme was life in German-occupied Europe, for the conquerors and the conquered alike. One morning someone stole the diary. Nothing else. The police said it was a slick, professional job. We were all rather puzzled. It's not particularly valuable.'

'It was to someone,' Bergerac said grimly.

'So you've heard nothing about it?'

He shook his head. 'I've a faint idea why it might have been stolen; that's all.'

She raised her eyebrows in a question.

'Nullhausen worked with a Vichy Frenchman called Patrice Marigny – '

Dr Godly grinned. 'The famous ghost?'

'That's the one. We've just heard that the real Marigny is dead. He was almost certainly killed by a professional Nazi-hunter called Dulov. Dulov is probably on Jersey right now. I think he's looking for something. I think it's something that Marigny left behind in 1945. I thought maybe this diary – ah, what's the use? It looks like Dulov had the same idea.'

Dr Godly bounced in her seat. She looked about sixteen. 'But you don't need the original, do you? You realize we've got a photocopy?'

She was out of the office before Bergerac had time to reply. He heard her rummaging in the room next door.

Seconds later, she returned with a buff-coloured envelope file.

'Can I borrow that?' Bergerac asked.

She grinned at him. 'You read German, then? Even if you do, you'd find Nullhausen's home-made shorthand a bit of a problem.'

'There's no translation?'

She shook her head. 'But I can translate it for you.'

'I need it now.'

'We'll do it now. It won't take long. I presume you're really only interested in the entries that concern Henry Tillersland.'

'How did you know that?' Bergerac snapped.

'You *are* a suspicious sergeant. According to the *Post*, George Crozier and Miss Irefield believed Marigny's ghost was linked with Tillersland. Actually, I've been expecting Miss Irefield on the same errand as you.'

'Miss Irefield is dead.'

The smile left Dr Godly's face. 'She used to come and use our library – she was writing a book about Jersey ghosts. I . . . I felt rather sorry for her, actually. How did it happen?'

'She appears to have fallen over a cliff.'

'Appears?'

'That's what I said.' Bergerac hesitated an instant. 'Her camera fell over too. We developed the film inside it. There was a picture of Marigny.'

'Of a *ghost*?'

'I don't think I believe in ghosts.'

Dr Godly stared at him. 'No, of course you don't.' She tapped the file on her lap. 'You think there's a connection?'

'I don't know yet.' Bergerac tried to avoid the distracting sight of Dr Godly's legs; although she was a small woman, the legs seemed to go on for ever. 'Could we get on with the diary? Sorry, but I'm in a hurry.'

She sighed. 'Pity about that. Still, perhaps you're not always so rushed?'

Bergerac nodded. 'Not always.' He squared his conscience by telling himself that Dr Godly's co-operation was professionally essential. He wondered what her first name was.

'Poor old Nullhausen,' she began. 'All he ever wanted to be was Hamburg's answer to PC Plod. I'll tell you a bit about him first.'

As she talked, Bergerac felt increasingly sympathetic towards Nullhausen. He bore no relation to the stereotypical Gestapo officer; he was just an ordinary copper who, moved by a bureaucratic accident to a job he hated, was desperately trying to keep his nose clean.

The diary was his insurance policy against Germany losing the war. Dr Godly read out the entries that dealt with Tillersland's arrest. Nullhausen had not been present at the man's interrogation and death; his relief was obvious – and so was his bewilderment. *Why*, he wrote, *is Marigny running so big a risk with the end of the war in sight?*

In his way, Nullhausen had been a good policeman: he sniffed around until he found the answer. Marigny, he noted, had spent the day after Tillersland's death searching the house at Wellington Road with quite exceptional thoroughness. According to the gorilla whom Marigny had taken with him, they had even prised up the floorboards.

Nullhausen, meanwhile, was doing a little research of his own. He discovered that Marigny had recently interviewed several officials at Lloyds Bank but had left no record of the subject of his discussions. Nullhausen questioned the same officials and found out that Marigny had been asking about Tillersland's assets – in particular about a van Gogh he had owned. The bank believed that the picture was now in England; Marigny, it seemed to Nullhausen, was not so sure.

Dr Godly looked up. 'A van Gogh – do you think that's what Dulov is after?'

Bergerac shrugged. 'Your guess is as good as mine. Did Marigny find it?'

'Nullhausen thinks not. Marigny vanished just before the end of the war. Nullhausen thought he'd got an escape route lined up. Maybe he vanished into the ranks – disguised himself as a sick soldier or something. He was a clever man.'

'That's obvious enough. Presumably the van Gogh was just the icing on the cake as far as he was concerned.'

'How do you mean, Sergeant? Must I call you Sergeant, by the way? It sounds so formal. My name's Jenny.'

'I'm Jim.' Bergerac swallowed: their relationship was developing rather too quickly for his liking. 'To go back to Marigny: he was a wealthy man when he died, and obscurity itself doesn't come cheap. The odds are, he did a lot of looting during the war, both here and in France.' He glanced at his watch and allowed himself the luxury of an irrelevant question. 'What happened to Nullhausen in the end?'

'He didn't have much luck. Gretl – that was his wife – was killed in the bombing. When he got back to Hamburg, the British Military Government gave him a rough time because of his Gestapo connections. After all his effort, no one took the diary seriously. He ended up as a builder's labourer. He died in what they call straitened circumstances in '53. The diary was auctioned after his death and someone bought it for us.'

'It doesn't seem fair, does it?'

Jenny Godly put the file on her desk. 'He picked the losing side.'

'You could say the losing side picked him.' Bergerac stood up. 'Well, thanks for your help, Dr – er, Jenny.'

'I suppose what you're really wondering is who the informant was.'

'What makes you say that?'

She smiled up at him. 'It's obvious, isn't it? Nullhausen thought Marigny was having an affair with one of Tillersland's servants; that was how he knew so much about Tillersland. Not just the van Gogh – the radio and the Jewish mother too. And Nullhausen said that someone unlocked the gates for them when they came to arrest Tillersland. So that means the traitor was either Elsie Fishguard or Marie Crozier.'

'Very likely.' Bergerac turned towards the door. Dr Godly was inconveniently bright – no doubt about that; she had reached the same conclusion as soon as he had. 'Now, if you'll excuse me – '

'And someone in the present,' she continued inexorably, 'is looking for the van Gogh. Not just Dulov – but someone who looks like Marigny used to look in the war. So . . .'

Bergerac looked round as Jenny Godly hesitated. She had joined him by the door; she was close enough for him to smell her perfume.

'So?' he said.

'Maybe Marigny had a son. He'd be about the same age now as Marigny was then – early forties.' She hesitated again. 'The old man who saw Marigny's ghost – wasn't that *George* Crozier?'

Bergerac nodded unwillingly.

'Marie's husband, I presume. And isn't their son a Chief Inspector or something?'

'Look, Jenny – can I ask you a favour?' Bergerac realized she was only an inch away from him now. He edged away.

She edged after him. 'Anything you like, Jim.'

'Don't mention this to anyone yet. And keep Nullhausen's diary under wraps. Don't get me wrong: this isn't a cover-up or anything like that. But at present it's all rather sensitive.'

'All right.' The tip of Jenny's tongue ran along her lips.

'But on one condition. When this is over, you take me out to dinner and tell me all about it.'

'It's a deal,' Bergerac said.

The sensation was unpleasantly and mysteriously familiar.

While he waited, Barney Crozier tried to recall why it was familiar. He was sitting on a hard chair. A typewriter tapped behind him. The room felt like an institution because of the pervasive smell of floor polish.

Floor polish – that was it. It reminded him of school. To be more precise, it reminded him of sitting in the secretary's office outside the headmaster's study. A prefect had caught him smoking behind the bicycle sheds. Whatever happened, the consequences were going to be bad. If the headmaster was feeling lenient, he would be caned; if the old man was in a vicious mood, it might end in expulsion.

The intercom buzzed on the secretary's desk. She looked up.

'The Superintendent will see you now, sir.'

Inside the office four armchairs had been drawn up round the coffee-table. They were all there – the Superintendent who was Crozier's immediate superior; the Chief Officer who was such a rarefied functionary that ordinary mortals scarcely ever saw him; and Charlie Hungerford who, in his capacity as chairman of the Law and Order Committee, could be relied upon to stick his nose in where he wasn't wanted.

Hungerford was the first to speak. 'For God's sake, man – you look like death warmed up.'

'Sit down, Barney,' the Superintendent said quietly. He was a slow-moving and slow-speaking man, whose mind was probably quicker than anyone else's there.

The Chief Officer said nothing. He rationed his words as if he had to pay for them himself.

'You don't look well,' the Superintendent went on. 'You shouldn't have come in.'

Crozier sat down on the edge of the chair. He glanced across the table at the Superintendent, the only man present who was likely to understand.

'I've done something rather foolish, sir,' he said. 'That's why I asked for this meeting. You may wish to suspend me from duty. Or perhaps it'd be better all round if I resigned.'

'Come on, Barney,' Hungerford said. 'I dare say it's not as bad as all that. We're all friends here, eh? I always say – '

The Superintendent overrode Hungerford by ignoring him. 'You'd better let us decide that,' he said to Crozier. 'What's the problem?'

'I'm being blackmailed.' Once the word was out Crozier felt strangely distanced from everything that was happening. Relief detached him from his surroundings. 'I've had two anonymous phone calls in the last few days. At first the caller – ah – put pressure on me concerning a private matter. But in the second call, the demand affected my professional life, which is why I'm here now. To be specific, I was advised to treat Miss Irefield's death as an accident.'

'Who's got that case?' the Superintendent asked. 'Jim Bergerac?'

Crozier nodded.

'Have you put any pressure on him?'

'Last night I . . . I didn't exactly encourage a certain line of his investigation. I haven't seen him this morning.'

The Chief Officer spoke for the first time: 'And what is the blackmailer's lever against you, Chief Inspector?'

'I'm sorry, sir – I can't tell you that.'

'Can't or won't?'

'Won't.'

The room was silent apart from the muffled sound of the typewriter next door. The Chief Officer gave an almost imperceptible shrug.

The Superintendent stirred in his chair. 'What made you decide to tell us, Barney?'

Crozier cleared his throat. 'After the second call – which came just before I went home yesterday evening – I realized that this couldn't go on, since it would have a direct effect on my work as a police officer.' He moistened his lips, which were suddenly dry. *How long will I be a police officer?* 'I discussed the matter with my wife before I phoned you last night to request this meeting.'

Someone else seemed to be saying these words. Someone standing in a witness box. Or in the dock.

Hungerford coughed and said, more in sorrow than in anger, 'I must say I'm rather surprised that you took so long to report this to us. You've been under a lot of strain, I know, what with Richard doing a vanishing trick and so on. Still, you could have come and seen me in private, Barney, or – '

'All right,' the Superintendent said. 'We'll talk about this later. Barney, I want you to go home.'

'On what basis, sir?'

'We'll call it compassionate leave. For the moment.'

Peggy Masters answered the phone on the second ring.

'Peggy? Is Jim Bergerac there?'

She recognized the Superintendent's voice immediately. 'I'm afraid not, sir. He's on duty, but he hasn't been in this morning.'

'Well, where is he?'

'I don't know. He hasn't called in. And we have no record of his planned movements.'

'I see.'

There was an ominous silence on the other end of the line. Officers were supposed to stay in touch with headquarters at all times.

'Peggy, Chief Inspector Crozier is going home on compassionate leave, with immediate effect. As soon as you see Bergerac, tell him I want him upstairs. Got that?'

'Yes, sir.'

*

There were two pubs in the village, one at either end.

Arkwright chose the one that looked more prosperous. The bar was crammed with fake Jacobean settles and horse brasses. It was just after midday. A large, bearded man was sitting at the table in the window, reading a newspaper. Apart from him, the only customers were two plump men who were propping up the bar: they were on the far side of middle age and both had bags under their bloodshot eyes. Many people retired to Jersey for the privilege of drinking themselves to death in pleasant surroundings with the additional advantage of a twenty-five per cent rate of income tax. And the alcohol was cheap too.

'Funny business,' one of them was saying. 'I always said she was off her rocker.' He looked broodingly into his whisky, nodding his head. 'You often get it in women of that age. Unmarried ones especially. Take it from me, old boy.'

'Aye,' his companion said. 'Your round, isn't it?'

Arkwright waited while they ordered. Both of them studied him covertly. Today he was safe in the dark glasses and a new coat and hat.

When it was his turn, he asked for a large gin and tonic. 'There seems to be a lot of police activity today,' he said to no one in particular. 'Anything happened?'

'One of our local eccentrics fell over a cliff,' the first man said. 'She was a bit – ' he tapped his head – 'if you get my meaning.'

The second man put his glass down on the counter with great care. 'Aye,' he said.

As an actor, Arkwright was sensitive to voices. The first man was trying for a vaguely Sandhurst effect, perhaps to match the vaguely military moustache; but the Midlands vowels kept obtruding. Arkwright adjusted his own voice to give a rather better imitation of an officer and a gentleman.

'An accident, I presume?'

'Of course – what else? Harmless old biddy, but definitely round the twist. Believed in ghosts, you know. Just the type to take a midnight stroll over the edge of a cliff – eh, Doug?'

Doug's glass was now empty. 'Aye,' he said.

Arkwright sipped his gin. 'Rather sad, I suppose.'

'These things happen, old chap,' the first man said cheerfully. 'Gives the police something to do – they spend most of their time sitting around on their backsides, waiting for the salaries we pay them.'

'They seem to be making quite a meal of it.'

Doug stirred. 'Same again, Chris?' He nodded to the barman without waiting for an answer.

'I was chatting to one of the bobbies,' Chris went on. 'If you ask me, they just wanted a chance to play with their new toys. It's amazing, the gadgetry they have these days. A lot of fuss about nothing, if you ask me. They'll be leaving this afternoon.'

'Oh, really?' Arkwright said. He turned to Doug. 'Let me get those.'

'You're a gentleman, sir,' Chris said. 'Not a resident, are you? Just passing through?'

'Yes,' Arkwright said. 'That's it.'

CHAPTER
17

The house looked west over La Moye golf course.

Usually Leonard Silbermann crawled up the drive as slowly as he could. This was partly because travelling at speed increased the risk of a chip of gravel marring the immaculate paintwork of the Ferrari. The main reason was that the view, the gardens and the long, white house were a source of pleasure to him. They gave him a yardstick with which to measure his progress in the last fifty years. He had come a long way from a rat-infested flat in Whitechapel.

This afternoon, however, neither the view nor the paintwork delayed him. He skidded to a halt at the front of the house and ran inside. His wife was in the hall, arranging flowers.

'You're early, Len.' She came towards him to receive the usual kiss. 'Would you like some tea?'

He fended her off. 'Where's Fisher?'

'Jerome? He's pottering round the garden. But what's up?'

Silbermann ignored her. He darted outside and searched the grounds, cursing the landscape gardener who had persuaded him to have so many winding paths and hidden corners. He would have liked to call out, but there was a danger that the neighbours might hear.

Dulov was sitting on the low stone wall that surrounded an ornamental pond, watching the goldfish. It was a fine afternoon and he was in his shirt-sleeves. He looked up and smiled at Silbermann.

'You promised me there'd be no trouble,' Silbermann hissed.

'Trouble, Leonard?' Dulov repeated in a lazy voice. 'How could there be trouble on such a beautiful day?'

'Yosef, *please*. This is important. Two men from the Bureau des Etrangers came to the office. They know we do business for you, though God knows how.'

'Through the bank, probably,' Dulov said. 'It doesn't matter.'

'But it does matter that they know you're on the island. And it's worse than that, much worse.' Silbermann's legs gave way. He sat down on the wall beside Dulov and opened his briefcase. 'Here. Today's *Post*.'

Dulov took the newspaper and shook it open.

'CLIFF DEATH DEEPENS GESTAPO MYSTERY,' Silbermann said. 'And on the next page: JERSEY POLICE SEEK NAZI-HUNTER. Oh, my God. So that's what you were up to last night.'

Dulov studied the photograph at the head of the first item. 'It really is a remarkable likeness. It's a son, I imagine.'

'They know you killed Marigny! We have an extradition treaty with Spain. There's a warrant for your arrest.'

Dulov was still absorbed in the photograph. 'So that's who it was,' he murmured. 'The competition, you might say.'

'Did you go to the cottage?'

'Me? What makes you think that?'

'You were out most of last night, Yosef. Her address was mentioned in the article about Marigny's ghost.' Silbermann's control snapped and his voice rose to a shriek. '*Did you kill her?*'

'Hush, Leonard. I was only having a look round – it used to be Tillersland's cottage, you see. I was very unlucky. The other man was there too, and he heard me sneeze. That didn't really matter, but the woman was taking

162

photographs. I thought I was in one of them. So I pushed her over. It was the only thing to do. I thought the camera went with her. Unfortunately, the man ran away before I could deal with him. But that's only a temporary difficulty. There's no way he could have seen my face.'

His tone was low and reasonable. For a moment Silbermann almost allowed himself to be soothed. Then outrage and fear welled up again.

'You can't do that sort of thing here,' he said.

'Why not? You are happy enough to benefit from my – ah – executions when they take place in other countries. What's the difference?'

'Damn it, I live here. And you're staying with me.'

'Yes, I agree.' Dulov patted Silbermann's arm. 'It is a little riskier, but on the other hand the stakes are higher. For both of us.'

'What do you mean?'

'I shall find the van Gogh. It's an unusual work. It has appreciated in value far more than Marigny could have hoped. When I killed him, he pretended he *knew* it was at the cottage – did I tell you that? He was trying to buy his life with it. Ironic, really; of course, he didn't know that I had got Nullhausen's diary. He was only guessing the painting was there. Still, he may have been right. Tillersland had to hide it somewhere, and the cottage is the obvious place.'

'Then why didn't he look there himself?'

'Because the military fortified that area in 1943, and they took over the cottage. In April and May '45, with an invasion looming, even a Gestapo officer couldn't turf them out.'

'If the painting is there,' Silbermann said slowly, 'and if you find it, and if all goes well, what sort of money are we talking about?'

Dulov shrugged. 'It's hard to be precise in these things. On the open market, my estimate is that *The Butcher* would fetch at least $20 million. Of course, in the circumstances, we shall have to settle for rather less.'

Silbermann licked his lips. 'Then how much?'

'I have three private buyers lined up. They'll bid against each other if they have to. I'll be disappointed if we don't clear fifteen.'

'And?'

Dulov's eyes were amused. 'Your commission, you mean? In this case, I think we should raise it to twenty per cent. No – why should I haggle with you, my friend? Twenty-five per cent. You deserve no less.'

'Good God.' Silbermann was silent. He told himself that he was professionally used to the high-risk, high-return philosophy. And $3.75 million was a very high return indeed.

'The police,' Dulov went on, 'will not be at the cottage for ever. I very much doubt if they have enough evidence to justify a murder investigation. They know nothing of the van Gogh. For the time being, I am quite safe here. The police have no reason to suspect you. I'll keep out of the way of your daily woman. Your wife won't talk.'

'But how will you get off the island?'

'Always the worrier, my friend.' Dulov's smile took the sting from the words. 'I have another passport – a French one. I can change my appearance. The best thing will be to join a party of day-trippers from St Malo. Do you have any other worries?'

Silbermann stared at the ground. 'The other man, Yosef – the one who looks like Marigny. He'll be waiting for the police to leave the cottage. What happens if . . .'

'That's nothing for you to bother about.' Dulov patted Silbermann's hand. 'You can leave him entirely to me.'

CHAPTER
18

When Bergerac had finished speaking, the Superintendent said nothing for thirty seconds. His capacity for silence was one of the more formidable weapons in his armoury.

Bergerac tried not to squirm in his chair.

'There are three main points I want to make,' the Superintendent said at last. 'One: Barney Crozier came up here this morning, said he was being blackmailed and wanted to resign. You underestimated his honesty, Jim. He wouldn't give us any details on the blackmail. I sent him home on compassionate leave.'

'I'm glad,' Bergerac said. 'Do you agree that it's probable that someone's saying that Marie Crozier was Marigny's mistress?'

The Superintendent gave the smallest of nods.

'And maybe that Barney himself is Marigny's bastard?'

'Have you checked that out?'

'Yes, sir. I looked up the records. Barney was born in January '46. Now, George was in the first batch of British troops, the Hampshires, to reach the island, early in May '45. If he was the father, then Barney was born a little prematurely. It's perfectly possible. The blackmailer is probably saying that Marie Crozier conceived a few weeks earlier. But, of course, that's a lie.'

'Why, Jim?'

'Because we've got a photo of Marigny's bastard – alive and well and on the island. We can only assume he's the blackmailer – primed by his mother, Elsie Fishguard, with all the facts about Tillersland, the Croziers and Marigny.'

'You'd better see Barney and get confirmation. Tell him I want him back on duty by tomorrow morning. That's one point. Number two: for the moment, you're in charge of both sides of this case – Dulov and the Fishguards. The Chief Officer and the Committee, not to mention Special Branch, Interpol and the Spanish police' – the Superintendent permitted himself a small smile – 'are anxious to see this matter sorted out. Not to put too fine a point on it, some of them are getting hysterical. None of that need bother you too much. But what does concern you is Miss Irefield: it's a virtual certainty that she was murdered, and I want her killer. And fast.'

'Yes, sir. And your third point?'

'Ah, yes.' The Superintendent stared across the desk, his eyes expressionless. 'If you go AWOL once more when you're meant to be on duty, I'll have you disciplined. In fact, I'll throw the book at you. Is that clear? You're a policeman, remember, not the Lone Ranger.'

'We've been over the whole place with a fine-tooth comb, Jim. Over.'

Reception was bad, and Bergerac signalled to Peggy to turn up the volume on the R/T. They were in the main office of the Bureau.

'Terry?' he said. 'Can you describe your mysterious stranger? Over.'

'Five-nine or five-ten; lightly built. Wearing sunglasses. Clean-shaven. Navy-blue raglan overcoat – looked new. Dark hair, but difficult to see much because he kept his hat on all the time.'

DC Goddard came into the office. Bergerac waved him over as he spoke into the microphone.

'You're sure about what he was doing?'

'He squeezed a lot of gossip out of the two old soaks in the bar,' Wilson said over a background of static. 'Almost all about Miss Irefield and the state of the police investigation. Maybe it was innocent, but I doubt it. Over.'

Bergerac glanced at his watch: it was 3.15. 'I want the scene-of-the-crime boys to pull out on schedule – and lock up the cottage. But you stay behind. Discreetly. The best place for a stake-out would be the edge of that little wood: you can watch the road, the path and the cottage itself from there. I don't think they'll try anything by daylight, but you never know. You're watching for Dulov and/or the man Miss Irefield photographed. We think they're rivals. Radio in at twenty-minute intervals. OK? We'll get you a back-up team as soon as possible, but it may take time – we're fully stretched here. But in any case, I'll join you about five – earlier if I can. Over.'

'I read you. Over and out.'

Bergerac turned to Peggy and Goddard. His tiredness had been swamped by a surge of adrenalin.

'Barry, check out a Mrs Elsie Fishguard this end. She'll be in her seventies now. Probably island-born; married; worked as a live-in servant for Henry Tillersland while her husband was away in the war. You know the routine – family, form, if any, financial status. We're especially interested in a son who must be in his early forties by now. I don't think either of them is still a resident, but you never know.'

'Right, Jim.' Goddard hovered, waiting to hear more.

Bergerac jerked his head at the door. 'Off you go.' He turned to Peggy. 'Meanwhile, you get on to the Met with the same set of questions. It's more than possible that Mrs Fishguard left the island after the war. Twist their arms if you have to – we're in a hurry. If you have any problems, call Special Branch and tell them Dulov's involved with the Fishguards; they'll back you all the way.'

Peggy blinked. 'Yes, Jim. Incidentally, Charlie Hungerford phoned and wanted to – '

'Phone him back later and say I'll be in touch. Next week, if he's lucky.'

'Jim!'

'And another thing, Peggy: get on to Claude Yves. Tell him from me that the police are now treating Miss Irefield's death as an accident. He can quote "reliable police sources" if he wants. I need the news on Radio Jersey and in the *Post*.'

'All right.' Peggy scribbled furiously on her shorthand pad. 'There was another call for you while you were upstairs with the Superintendent – a Dr Godly. She said it was something arising from your meeting this morning.'

The alluring thought of Jenny Godly momentarily distracted Bergerac from the matter in hand. He wondered if the 'something arising' was rather too personal to be relayed through a third person.

'I'll phone her later,' he said coldly. 'If you need me, I'll be at Barney Crozier's.'

Bergerac could ill afford the time, but it had to be done.

He parked in the drive and rang the doorbell. Alice answered the door and showed him into the sitting-room.

A family conference was in full swing. George was there, and so was Richard, who was staring unhappily at the carpet. Barney Crozier was standing by the window.

Bergerac came straight to the point. 'Your mother wasn't Marigny's mistress. Elsie Fishguard was.'

'What the hell – ' Barney began. He stopped abruptly and then said, 'Jim, are you sure? Really sure?'

The next half-hour turned into a bewildering question-and-answer session. None of the Croziers knew the full story; but some knew more than others. Barney eventually produced the photograph that had been the opening shot of the blackmailing campaign.

George pounced on it. 'Of course that's not your mother,' he said triumphantly.

'Well, it looked like those old pictures of her,' Barney said, 'and – '

'It's Elsie Fishguard, boy. Do you think I don't recognize her? I know they looked alike, but they weren't the same, inside or out. Do you think I don't know my own wife?'

'But Dad – she's wearing the garnet brooch. The one you gave Alice.'

'There's nothing odd about that,' Alice interrupted. 'Elsie and Marie were living in the same house. Women are always borrowing things from each other.'

George tapped the photo. 'If you'd shown me this right away, you could have saved yourself a lot of trouble.'

'But I couldn't,' Barney said with a spurt of exasperation. He added in a gentler voice, 'What if it *had* been my mother?'

There was a moment's silence. It occurred to Bergerac that Crozier, probably the most ambitious man in the Jersey States Police, had been prepared to jeopardize his entire career rather than hurt his father's feelings. It was a refreshing sidelight on his character.

'Elsie Fishguard?' Richard said suddenly. 'She'd be an old woman, right? In her seventies?'

Bergerac nodded.

'And she was the blackmailer?'

'Yes.' Bergerac frowned. 'Do you think you know her?'

Once Richard started talking, the words tumbled out in a torrent. The woman he knew as Mrs Smilie was clearly Elsie Fishguard, and the son was Marigny's bastard. Bergerac took a description; he would have it circulated on an all-island alert as soon as he got back to headquarters. The crucial question no one could answer was what was in the letter from Tillersland to his son.

George lit his pipe. 'Well, this is all interesting,' he said between puffs. 'You know something, Jim? I never liked that Elsie. I wouldn't be surprised if she had a bad aura.'

Bergerac coughed. 'Maybe. Look, George – I must be off.'

'Nothing to report,' Terry Wilson said. 'Over and out.'

He switched off the radio and slid it into the pocket of his duffel coat. He was lying in a dip in the ground, sheltered on one side by a straggling elder tree and on the other by a yew. It was ten past four; the afternoon was still fine, but it was becoming appreciably chillier. It was impossible to get completely out of the wind.

The cold was beginning to creep into his limbs. It was a pity that Jim hadn't given him more warning. Outdoor surveillance could be marginally less unpleasant if you had the time to pad yourself with an extra set of clothes and to fill a thermos with coffee.

He sat up and rubbed his hands vigorously together. He wished that Jim had briefed him more fully. This was a weird case and no mistake. It was at that moment that he heard a distant tapping.

It was a regular noise, like a heartbeat or the steady drip of water. It came from the direction of the road. As he listened, it grew gradually louder.

An old lady emerged over the brow of the hill, some thirty yards from Wilson. Obviously frail, she carried a white stick, which tapped against the tarmac at every step. Her head nodded from side to side as she walked. She had taken trouble with her appearance: she wore a smart, fawn-coloured wool coat and a bright headscarf. Even at this distance, Wilson could see the slash of scarlet lipstick that outlined her mouth. She moved slowly along the line of the fence towards the gate.

Wilson was in a quandary. The old woman was obviously not a sightseer – not that you'd expect many of those at this time of year; it was equally obvious that she could have nothing to do with this case. Probably a local, or else she would have come by car; he wondered if she was a friend of Miss Irefield's.

One thing was certain: she couldn't stay here. They couldn't afford an innocent bystander if Dulov or Marigny's ghost put in an appearance. The risk outweighed the disadvantage of breaking cover. It wouldn't take long.

He stood up, fumbling for his warrant card. The old lady had reached the gate by now. Wilson walked out of the copse, making no attempt to conceal himself, and strode across the road to intercept her.

'Excuse me, madam,' he said, loudly in case she was deaf. 'I'm a police officer. May I ask what you're doing here?'

The old lady turned. She looked so feeble that Wilson almost took her by the arm. The make-up on her face was a brave but doomed attempt to conceal the ravages of age.

'A policeman, madam,' he repeated. 'Would you like to see my warrant card?'

She held out a trembling hand for it and studied it for a long moment. He wondered if the eyes behind the thick glasses were capable of reading it.

'Were you a friend of Miss Irefield?' he asked.

'Oh, yes, officer, an old friend. So sad that she passed on.'

'Was there something you wanted?'

She nodded. 'Yes, there is.'

In that last second Wilson knew that something was wrong. Something in her eyes, maybe, or in her voice; perhaps a muscle twitched in that wrinkled, powdered face.

But his knowledge came too late.

The blow caught him just above his right ear. The old woman's painted lips twitched a smile. It was the last thing he remembered.

CHAPTER
19

The information was waiting in Bergerac's in-tray when he got back into the Bureau.

He flicked through it: a stack of sheets from the teleprinter, mug shots, fingerprints, photocopies of press cuttings, a bundle of neatly typed memos and several pages of notes in Goddard's appalling handwriting. It was a relief to have incontrovertible proof that the Fishguards were neither ghosts from the past nor creatures of his own imagination: they were living flesh and blood.

'You've done marvels, Peggy.'

She smiled primly. 'I'm afraid we're not very popular in London. I had to invoke Special Branch.'

Bergerac grinned. He pitied the records clerk who got on the wrong side of Peggy Masters when she felt that she was in the right.

'Get me some coffee, will you?' he asked. 'I'll have a look at these.'

'Oh, by the way – Dr Godly phoned again. No message.'

'Good,' Bergerac said.

He looked at his watch. He would have to hurry if he was going to reach Elizabeth Cottage by five. There was a lot of information to plough through. Bergerac sorted through it, piecing together the disjointed facts and linking them with inferences. A coherent narrative began to emerge. Goddard's material wasn't much use – either they knew it already or it was irrelevant. The real story began after the war.

Elsie Fishguard had moved to London with her husband late in 1945. They separated almost immediately and divorced a few years later. A son, Winston, was born on 25 November 1945. Maybe Fishguard objected to bringing up another man's bastard. Elsie remarried as soon as the divorce came through. Her new husband, Robert Arkwright, deserted her after two years; but his wife and stepson retained his surname.

Both Elsie and Winston had criminal records – and so, for that matter, had Robert Arkwright; that was why the Met had so much information on them. Arkwright, now deceased, had been a pimp with black-market connections. There was little doubt that he had introduced Elsie to the game; she had several convictions for soliciting.

Winston Arkwright had other interests. From grammar school he had won a scholarship to RADA, but he had never fulfilled his early promise as an actor. He had done several seasons with a provincial repertory company; he had carried a spear for the RSC; he had done a few voice-overs for advertisements; and, to crown his career, a television advertisement for a dandruff shampoo had made him briefly familiar to an audience of millions. For the last few years he had been unemployed.

For the rest, Winston had five convictions – one for theft, one for house-breaking and three for minor drug offences. In all, he had served fifteen months in gaol.

Bergerac turned to the photographs. Marigny's face stared up at him: the off-duty clown was no ghost but a petty crook. The Met had come up with a recent picture of the mother: it was an interesting face – hard and careworn on the surface, but with a good bone structure underneath. If Richard Crozier could positively identify her, they would have no problem at all.

'Jim?' It was Goddard's voice behind him.

'What is it?'

'It's 4.35. Terry hasn't called in.'

Bergerac looked up, surprised the time had passed so quickly. Wilson usually made a fetish of punctuality. 'When was he due?'

'4.30. I tried to raise him, but I couldn't get an answer.'

Bergerac was already on his feet. 'I'm going over there.' He jostled into Peggy, spilling the coffee she was bringing him. 'Follow me as soon as you can,' he said over his shoulder. 'I want at least three men with you. And Peggy – put out an all-island alert for the Arkwrights and Dulov.'

The door slammed behind him.

Peggy, unsure what was happening, looked at Goddard. 'Do *you* want some coffee?'

'We should have waited, Mother,' Winston Arkwright said.

'And risk the other man getting here first? Stop wasting time.'

'Dulov? If the newspaper's got it right, he's – well – a professional. Don't you think we should – '

'That bastard killed Patrice,' she said savagely. 'You know what I'm going to do with my share of the money? Put a contract on him.'

Arkwright shook his head but said nothing. He would never understand women. Marigny had deserted his mother in 1945, leaving her with nothing but an unwanted baby in her belly. He had ignored her for over forty years. Yet still she wanted to pay good money to have his murderer killed.

'Come on,' his mother said.

'I was wondering – '

'If you had a penny for every second thought you've had, you'd be a bloody millionaire.'

Arkwright shrugged. He was out of breath. The copper was a big man, and it had been a real effort to drag him down the path to the cottage. They smashed the kitchen window; Arkwright climbed in and opened the back door from the inside.

The copper was now lying on his side, half under the big table. His face was a nasty colour, but he was still breathing. The hair above his right ear was matted with blood where Arkwright had hit him with the monkey-wrench. They had trussed him up with a clothes line.

'He'll be all right, won't he?' Arkwright said. 'We don't want him to die on us.'

'Get on with it, Winston. Try the loft first. It's the obvious place for kids to hide.' His mother rummaged in the drawer in the table and found a kitchen knife with a wooden handle and a four-inch blade. 'I'll keep an eye on the sleeping beauty while I poke around in here.'

Arkwright found the entrance to the loft on the tiny landing. The ceiling was so low that a chair from Miss Irefield's bedroom gave him enough height to reach the hatch.

He hauled himself through the opening. Chinks of light showed between the slates. The loft was neither boarded nor insulated. He switched on his torch. A bird had nested in one corner. Over the years the spaces between the joists had filled up with debris – everything from dead spiders to builder's rubble. Arkwright scraped his hand along one of the spaces. You could easily hide a rolled-up painting there. And there were several trunks, a couple of cardboard boxes and a water tank. He would have to sift through the bloody lot. His new overcoat was already filthy.

While he searched, he grew steadily warmer. Soon he was unpleasantly hot. He would have stripped off his coat, but he didn't want to get his suit any dirtier than it already was. It was possible to stand up only in the middle of the loft, under the ridge-pole, so he spent most of his time on his hands and knees. No noises filtered up from below; he felt entirely alone.

As the temperature rose, so did his desperation. He blamed his mother for all this; he had always blamed his mother. When they found the van Gogh – *if* they found it –

the old cow would live to regret it. *He* was the one with the contacts on the fringes of the London art world; she would have to let him sell the painting. Once he had the money, it would be up to him how he used it. Supporting an aged parent – let alone splitting the profits with her – was not high on his list of priorities. Nor was putting a contract on Yosef Dulov.

And there wouldn't be a thing she could do about it. She could hardly complain to the Office of Fair Trading.

'Winston!'

Arkwright nearly lost his balance and put a foot between a pair of joists. The voice was directly beneath him. For one startled moment, it seemed to him that his mother could have been eavesdropping on his thoughts.

He crawled across the joists to the open hatch. His mother was standing below, peering up at him.

'Have you found it?' he asked excitedly.

'Come down,' she said. 'I've found something.'

Arkwright swung his legs through the opening. He lowered himself on to the seat of the chair. A shower of dust descended with him.

'What do you mean?' he said.

He turned round, automatically attempting to brush some of the dust from his sleeve.

'*Gently* does it,' a man said. 'Just stay there for a moment. We don't want any accidents, do we?'

The voice was low and pleasant. Something about the vowel sounds suggested that English was not the speaker's first language. The man was standing behind Arkwright's mother, half-way down the stairs.

Arkwright saw the gun before he saw the face. It was a .22 pistol, held in a gloved hand. In the Scrubs he had once shared a cell with a man who talked endlessly about guns. The .22 was the professional assassin's choice: it was small and it made very little noise, but, because of the small calibre, you only used it if you were near to your target and very confident of your aim.

Dulov.

'Clasp your hands together and rest them on your head. *Both of you.*'

Arkwright obeyed immediately. His mother took her time.

'You *do* look like your father,' Dulov said conversationally. 'Like he used to look, I mean. Get down off that chair and turn round.'

Arkwright's legs were shaking so much that he nearly fell over.

'Now you will both come downstairs. Slowly and backwards.'

'I can't walk backwards down them stairs,' Elsie Arkwright snapped. 'And I'll have to hold on to the rail.'

'As you wish,' Dulov said. 'But slowly. Very slowly.'

'Well, I'm not going to go fast, am I? Not at my age.'

The three of them descended to the kitchen. Dulov glanced at Wilson, who was still dead to the world, and ushered the Arkwrights into the sitting-room, where he lined them up facing the wall.

Winston cleared his throat. 'We . . . we don't have much time. The police may be here at any minute. Wouldn't it be wiser if we – ah – pooled our resources?'

'Shut up, Winston,' his mother hissed.

'What a good idea,' Dulov said. 'I much prefer to negotiate. I'm sure we are all reasonable people.'

'We have a letter,' Arkwright said eagerly, 'from Tillersland to his son.' One hand moved down and hovered beside the inside pocket of his jacket. 'It suggests that – '

'Stop!' Dulov barked. In a softer voice he went on: 'Let me get it.'

He extracted the letter and, keeping one eye on the Arkwrights, glanced through its contents.

'You take this to mean that Tillersland hid the van Gogh in the cottage?'

'Yes, of course,' Arkwright said. 'Or possibly in the grounds, I suppose.'

'And so we're looking for the children's "secret cache"?'

'The loft seemed – '

'*Be quiet!*' Dulov said. 'Listen.'

A car was coming up the hill.

The police? Arkwright didn't know whether he was glad or sorry. At least the police were unlikely to kill you.

Dulov darted to the window.

Out of the corner of his eye Arkwright saw a blur of movement and a flash of steel.

'*Mother!*' he screamed.

He was too late. Anyway, she never listened to him.

Dulov was already beginning to turn as Elsie Arkwright drove the kitchen knife into the side of his chest. His movement increased the force of the thrust.

His jacket was unbuttoned. The silk shirt offered little resistance to the knife. The blade slid between two ribs. Dulov's mouth was open; he didn't look hurt – he looked astonished.

Mrs Arkwright screamed with triumph. She twisted the knife in the wound and dragged it out. Dulov tried to hit her with the gun, but his arm moved in slow motion. Holding the knife with both hands, Elsie stabbed him again.

The gun fell to the floor.

Dulov's long limbs folded up like the legs of a collapsible tripod. He slithered to the floor. Winston Arkwright, his hands still clasped above his head, watched his mother drive the knife in, again and again. She sat astride her victim, working with the energy of rediscovered youth.

She glanced up at him. 'It's easy!' she said gleefully. 'Like cutting butter.' Suddenly her face changed. 'Get the gun, you fool.'

Arkwright stepped forward. It was strange there was so little blood and strange that a man like Dulov should, at the last resort, be so vulnerable to the blade of a small knife. Gingerly he picked up the gun. He was facing the window.

'Patrice,' his mother murmured rhythmicially behind him. 'Patrice. Patrice.'

The butt of the gun was still warm from Dulov's hand. It took a few seconds for Arkwright's mind to register what his eyes saw. A small blue car was parked on the road. One of the Japanese super-minis. Not an obvious police vehicle.

And then someone was knocking on the back door.

'Cooee!' a woman called. 'Is anyone at home?'

The Triumph Roadster jolted up the track in first gear. The engine whined as the wheels slipped, spraying the sides of the car with mud.

At one point a rusting oil drum, half concealed by the hedge, scraped along the side of the car. Finally a rut trapped both nearside wheels. There was an ominous clanking beneath the car. Suddenly the engine was much louder. Bergerac was dimly aware that the Triumph would need a new silencer as well as a respray.

He got out of the car and began to run. He had calculated that, if something *was* wrong at the cottage, it would be wiser not to give warning of his arrival. For that reason he had chosen to approach by the unmetalled path from the village.

The mud clung to his feet, making them twice as heavy as usual. It took him far longer to reach the copse than he had anticipated. Maybe he should have driven straight to the cottage after all. He half hoped that Terry Wilson would rise out of the undergrowth and challenge him.

But nothing was moving in the little wood. No birds

sang. The only sounds were the roar of the sea and a woman's voice, somewhere in the distance.

'Cooee! Is anyone at home?'

Arkwright straightened his tie and opened the door.

'Yes?' he said.

A small woman with blonde hair was standing on the doorstep. She was about thirty and extremely attractive.

'Who are you?' she demanded.

'Detective Constable Fishguard,' Arkwright said. 'And who are you?'

'I'm Dr Godly. I'm looking for Sergeant Bergerac. Is he here?'

Arkwright shook his head. *Dr* Godly – a police surgeon or something? He had been forced to open the door because if the woman looked through the downstairs windows she would see –

'Do you know where he is?'

'I'm afraid not, madam.' Arkwright realized he was sounding more like a butler than a detective constable. He injected a little roughness into his voice. 'I'd try headquarters if I were you. Or you can leave a message with me, if you like.'

He realized too late that she wasn't listening. She was staring through the gap between his body and the door jamb, and her eyes were widening with terror.

Oh, Christ – from there she must be able to see the copper's head with its halo of blood!

Arkwright grabbed the woman by the shoulders and dragged her into the kitchen. He kicked the door shut and pulled the .22 pistol from his waistband.

'You stupid bitch,' he said.

Yet again she wasn't listening to him. *No one ever listens to me . . .* This time she was staring through the doorway to the living-room. Her face was white. Suddenly she sat down on one of the hard chairs at the table. She covered her face with her hands.

'Oh, yes,' Arkwright said pettishly. 'It's real, you know. Not some bloody tableau vivant.'

He had automatically turned his back so he would not have to see what was in the other room. As Dulov's legs were in the way, he could not close the door. His mother, still astride the body, was rocking to and fro and moaning softly.

'She needs a doctor,' the woman said.

'She's got one, hasn't she?'

'I'm not a doctor of medicine. We must *do* something. You know, get help.'

Arkwright ignored her. He was thinking feverishly. It had all gone wrong. It was his mother's fault. He had to escape. It no longer mattered about the painting; maybe one day he would be able to come back.

The hired car was no use to him – it was parked half-way down the road to the village. He didn't have much money. But he had to get away. France would be safer than England – and nearer too. He glanced at the bowed head of the woman. For the first time he saw a gleam of hope.

Fortune had given him a hostage.

Arkwright grabbed her wrist and pulled her up. He showed her the gun and jabbed the muzzle in her side. She was too frightened even to strain away from him. That was pleasing. He had never had a gun in his hand before. It made him feel like a different person – stronger, somehow, and more decisive.

More like my father?

'You're driving me to the ferry,' he said. 'We're going to Brittany. Open the door and go out first. Walk slowly.'

Dr Godly obeyed him. She walked slowly outside, pausing on the path to look back at him. Arkwright followed her. As he passed through the doorway into the garden, two things happened.

Someone grabbed both the gun and his wrist, yanked him off his feet and sent him flying through the air.

And, just before he landed, Arkwright distinctly heard the wail of a police siren.

It was another long night.

The scene-of-the-crime team returned to the cottage. The police surgeon arrived for his preliminary investigation. Two ambulances were needed: one to take the body of Yosef Dulov to the mortuary, the other to ferry Terry Wilson and Elsie Arkwright – the former querulous and the latter heavily sedated – to the General Hospital.

The doctors wanted to keep Wilson under observation for twenty-four hours, but, according to the latest report, it was likely that he was suffering from nothing worse than a headache and severe damage to his professional self-esteem. Mrs Arkwright had been moved to the psychiatric unit. She was awake and talking now. The only problem was that she was having a conversation with Patrice Marigny in 1945.

At the Bureau, Bergerac worked through to the small hours. There were statements, interviews and too many cups of coffee. Arkwright wept and pleaded. It was all his mother's fault. Everything was her idea from start to finish. He had no idea that she had the kitchen knife concealed in the lining of her coat.

The Superintendent phoned just before midnight. Bergerac gave him his interim report.

At the end the Superintendent chuckled. 'Anyone with a grain of sense would have waited for back-up.'

'There wasn't time, sir. Arkwright could have got away, and we'd have had a high-speed car chase to cope with. With a gun in his hand, he was on some sort of emotional high. And there was Dr Godly to consider.'

'All right, Jim. Sometimes the Lone Ranger has his uses. Good-night.'

At 3.30 Bergerac decided that there was nothing more he could do for the next few hours. He picked up his jacket and walked wearily into reception.

A small figure was curled up on one of the sofas. You couldn't see the face – just a turned-up collar and a mass of blonde hair.

The desk sergeant coughed. 'She said she was waiting for you, Jim.'

Bergerac laid a hand on Dr Godly's shoulder and gave her a gentle shake.

She opened her eyes. 'Hello, Jim. Come to take me home?'

'I fixed up a squad car for you.'

'I told them you might need me for a second interview, so you'd be taking me back.'

She lived in St Lawrence, near the Dannemarche Reservoir. Bergerac's Triumph was still stuck in the mud below the copse, so he was driving an unmarked police car, which was normally used for surveillance work. For the first mile she said nothing.

At last Bergerac could stand it no more. 'Why did you really come out to the cottage?'

'I told you – I'd been researching the Tillerslands in our records. You know we've got back-files of all the local papers. In the thirties the old man was a sort of amateur gardening correspondent for the *Post*. He was always mentioning his little place in the country.'

'So you were coming to tell me you thought the picture was hidden there?'

'Exactly. And the letter you showed me, the one he left for his son, seems to confirm it.'

'Yes, but why – ?'

'I couldn't get through to you at the Bureau,' she rushed on, 'and I thought you might be up at the cottage, so – '

'Jenny – you could have left a message.'

'Yes, Jim,' she said. 'I know.' After a silence she added,

'You take the next left.' Another silence. 'It's the second bungalow on the right.'

He pulled over and stopped, leaving the engine running. She leant over him and switched off the engine.

'Come and have a drink or something.'

'I don't drink.'

'A cup of cocoa then. I've even got Horlicks. No Ovaltine, I'm afraid.'

'I only drink Ovaltine at this time of night.' Bergerac was conscious of her presence beside him. Too conscious. 'It's not going to work, Jenny. You're – we're trying to go too fast.'

'Is there someone else? You're not married, are you?'

'Not now. But there is someone else.'

'I've got an ex as well.' She tried to make a joke of it, but her voice would not obey her. 'It's another thing we have in common.'

'Don't tell me *you* haven't got a someone else?'

'As a matter of fact, I haven't,' she said angrily. 'Believe it or not, I'm choosy.'

'OK. I'm sorry.'

With a massive effort of will he kept his face turned away. He stared through the windscreen into the darkness, listening to her fast, shallow breathing and wondering if her skin was as smooth as it looked.

Jenny Godly kissed him on the cheek and opened the passenger door. 'I'm sorry too.' She climbed out of the car. 'Jim?'

'What?'

'I know quite a lot about furniture,' she said casually. 'It's one of my specialities. Did you notice the kitchen table at the cottage? The top is unusually thick for a farmhouse piece of that period.'

CHAPTER
20

'If you ask me,' George Crozier said, 'it all began with a man and a woman in a garden.' He winked at Bergerac. 'Just like the Book of Genesis, eh?'

'Come off it, Dad,' Barney said tartly. 'It was just – '

'I think I'll have the *Escalope de Saumon à l'Oseille*,' Alice interrupted; she was rather proud of her French accent. 'What shall we do about wine?'

'Count me out, love,' George said. 'I'll stick to Scotch.'

Barney shook his head over the menu. 'Have you seen the prices here?'

'You don't have to worry about that,' his father told him. 'This is my treat.'

'Nonsense. For a start, you can't afford it.'

'Yes, I can. I'm going to put the cottage on the market.'

Father and son glared at one another. It was a week after Dulov's death and the Arkwrights' arrest. There were six of them round the big table in Le Coq d'Or – Bergerac, Susan and four Croziers.

Richard Crozier sipped half a pint of lager and grinned shyly at Bergerac.

'Susan?' George said. 'Do you think Hobson and Young could handle the sale for me?'

'We'd love to. I'll do it myself.'

'Good.' George turned back to Barney. 'I want you and Alice to have the money – right away; no point in you hanging on till I kick the bucket. Mark you, I'll deduct the legal fees and Sue's commission and the cost of this dinner.'

'We . . . we can't accept that.'

185

'Why not? It'll be some consolation for that damned picture.'

There was a moment's silence. After Jenny Godly's tip-off, Bergerac had found the van Gogh. In 1940 Henry Tillersland had simply taken *The Butcher* out of its frame and wrapped it in oilskin. He then removed the top from the kitchen table at the cottage and screwed a tray, containing *The Butcher*, underneath it; finally he reassembled the table, sanded it down and gave the base a heavy coat of dark varnish. It was a simple hiding-place – but effective enough to keep its secret for over forty years. Under the wills of Henry Tillersland and Marie Crozier, the painting now belonged to George Crozier. And George didn't want it.

'I'll keep the table, though,' the old man went on. 'I often think of those three kids pretending it was a smugglers' cave.'

Crozier cleared his throat. 'You're absolutely sure about getting rid of the picture?'

His father nodded. 'I'm a socialist, boy – why should any one person own twenty million dollars' worth of paint and canvas? No – when they sort out the paperwork, it'll go to the nation. Maybe it'll give a few people some pleasure that way.'

'You're right,' Richard said suddenly. He looked at his father. 'Of *course* Grandad's right.'

George's face was serious. 'Besides, I don't think I want to own *The Butcher*. Have you noticed it lives up to its name? Three people have died because of it, maybe more.' He shivered. 'It's not lucky.'

There was another silence. For once neither Barney nor Alice felt inclined to accuse George of being superstitious.

Susan adroitly turned the conversation: 'What's this I hear about you selling a picture?' she asked Richard.

The boy flushed. 'It was all Jim's doing, really.'

Bergerac had arranged for a friend of his to look at a

portfolio of Richard's work. The friend ran what was probably the biggest art gallery in St Helier. Not only was the friend enthusiastic, but a visiting artist, whose name even Barney Crozier was familiar with, had happened to be in the gallery at the time and had made an offer for one of Richard's pictures.

'You going to try for art college then?'

He nodded. 'Our art teacher thinks I should.' He glanced at his parents and added, with the desperate simplicity of adolescence, 'If I don't, I'll spend the rest of my life regretting it.'

'Your gran would have been pleased,' George said.

Richard nodded; he was obviously a little embarrassed. 'I keep forgetting about your car,' he said to Bergerac. 'When do you want me to come over?'

'No need. It got a bit damaged up at the cottage. The police will pick up the tab. Or rather, the insurers will.'

'What's this?' Barney asked suspiciously.

'Richard was going to help me touch up the paintwork,' Bergerac said. 'Give me some technical advice. Smarten the car up a bit.'

'Maybe you could smarten yourself up while you're about it,' Crozier said.

'I thought I was looking quite respectable.' Bergerac glanced down at his suit and tie. 'I even polished my shoes before we came out.'

'I don't mean *now* – at the Bureau. Susan, can't you break into his wardrobe and burn that leather jacket of his? It makes him look like a teenage hoodlum.'

Susan shook her head. 'I wouldn't dare. He'd only be half a man without it.'

George drained his glass. 'Where's that waiter gone? I want to order.'

Bergerac glanced over his shoulder. All the waiters he could see were clustered round two new arrivals in the doorway.

'But I ordered the '73 Dom Pérignon!' a familiar voice said. 'You mean it's not on ice? I don't know what this place is coming to, I really don't.'

'Oh, no,' Barney muttered. 'Not Charlie.'

Hungerford surged into the restaurant. Peggy Masters was on his arm. He saw Bergerac and changed course for the Croziers' table.

'Well, this is a surprise,' he said, and his tone suggested that the surprise was not an altogether pleasant one. 'I didn't know that police salaries could stretch to Le Coq d'Or.'

'We've been saving up for a long time, Charlie,' Bergerac said. 'Sorry about the Dom Pérignon.'

'You'd think they'd get it right, wouldn't you? I mean, the prices they charge . . . Still, at least it keeps out the riff-raff.' Hungerford glanced at Bergerac and added, 'Usually. They say most of the *real* regulars are millionaires.'

George Crozier chuckled. '*I'm* a millionaire, now – just for a few days. I could probably buy you up, Charlie. Several times over, in fact.'

'Yes, well . . . There's a chap I wanted a word with . . .' Hungerford covered his confusion by hailing a waiter. 'Is Len Silbermann here tonight?'

'I'm afraid not, sir.'

'He won't be here for a while,' Crozier said. 'We arrested him this afternoon.'

'Len! Whatever for?'

'He was sheltering Dulov. There's not much doubt that he knew exactly what was going on. If nothing else, he's an accessory to Marigny's murder – after the fact, if not before.'

'Good God! You can't trust anyone these days.'

Peggy tugged Hungerford's arm. 'Our table's ready, Charles.'

'Why don't you join us?' George said. 'Plenty of room.'

'I don't think so, thanks,' Hungerford said quickly. 'Don't want to break up a family party.'

Peggy lingered for a moment. 'Oh, Jim – I nearly forgot. Dr Godly phoned just after you left the office. There was a message – something about Ovaltine now being in stock. I don't know what it means, but I hope it wasn't urgent.'

Bergerac knew that Susan was looking at him. There was a slight frown on her face.

'It doesn't matter, Peggy,' he said. 'Not urgent at all.'

FOR THE BEST IN PAPERBACKS, LOOK FOR THE

In every corner of the world, on every subject under the sun, Penguin represents quality and variety – the very best in publishing today.

For complete information about books available from Penguin – including Pelicans, Puffins, Peregrines and Penguin Classics – and how to order them, write to us at the appropriate address below. Please note that for copyright reasons the selection of books varies from country to country.

In the United Kingdom: For a complete list of books available from Penguin in the U.K., please write to *Dept E.P., Penguin Books Ltd, Harmondsworth, Middlesex, UB7 0DA*

In the United States: For a complete list of books available from Penguin in the U.S., please write to *Dept BA, Penguin, 299 Murray Hill Parkway, East Rutherford, New Jersey 07073*

In Canada: For a complete list of books available from Penguin in Canada, please write to *Penguin Books Canada Ltd, 2801 John Street, Markham, Ontario L3R 1B4*

In Australia: For a complete list of books available from Penguin in Australia, please write to the *Marketing Department, Penguin Books Australia Ltd, P.O. Box 257, Ringwood, Victoria 3134*

In New Zealand: For a complete list of books available from Penguin in New Zealand, please write to the *Marketing Department, Penguin Books (NZ) Ltd, Private Bag, Takapuna, Auckland 9*

In India: For a complete list of books available from Penguin, please write to *Penguin Overseas Ltd, 706 Eros Apartments, 56 Nehru Place, New Delhi, 110019*

In Holland: For a complete list of books available from Penguin in Holland, please write to *Penguin Books Nederland B.V., Postbus 195, NL–1380AD Weesp, Netherlands*

In Germany: For a complete list of books available from Penguin, please write to *Penguin Books Ltd, Friedrichstrasse 10 – 12, D–6000 Frankfurt Main 1, Federal Republic of Germany*

In Spain: For a complete list of books available from Penguin in Spain, please write to *Longman Penguin España, Calle San Nicolas 15, E–28013 Madrid, Spain*

Goodbye Soldier Spike Milligan

The final volume of his war memoirs in which we find Spike in Italy, in civvies and in love with a beautiful ballerina. 'Desperately funny, vivid, vulgar' – *Sunday Times*

The Nudists Guy Bellamy

Simon Venables, honeymooning under the scorching sun, has just seen the woman he should have married . . . 'It is rare for a book to be comic, happy and readable all at once, but Guy Bellamy's *The Nudists* is just that' – *Daily Telegraph*. 'Funny caustic and gloriously readable' – *London Standard*

I, Tina Tina Turner with Kurt Loder

'Tina Turner . . . has achieved the impossible; not one but two legends in her own lifetime' – *Cosmopolitan*. *I, Tina* tells the astonishing story that lies behind her success; electrifying, moving and unforgettable, it is one of the great life stories in rock-music history.

A Dark-Adapted Eye Barbara Vine

Writing as Barbara Vine, Ruth Rendell has created a labyrinthine journey into the heart of the Hillyard family, living in the respectable middle-class countryside after the Second World War. 'Barbara Vine has the kind of near-Victorian narrative drive that compels a reader to go on turning the pages' – Julian Symons in the *Sunday Times*

Survive! John Man

Jan Little, with her husband and daughter, escaped to the depths of the Brazilian jungle. Only she survived. Almost blind and totally alone, Jan Little triumphed over death, horror and desolation. Hers is a story of remarkable courage and tenacity.

A Man Made to Measure Elaine Crowley

Set in Dublin during the First World War, the story of *A Man Made to Measure* follows the fortunes of a group of people whose lives are changed forever by the fateful events of the Easter Uprising. 'Elaine Crowley writes like a dream . . . an exciting new discovery' – *Annabel*